From the diary of Maeve Elliott

Since she was a wee child, my granddaughter Scarlet has been surrounded by whirling winds. The spirit, as we say, runs high in that one. But even someone as wild as the Irish coast has her soft side. I see it in her.

I also see wistfulness. Perhaps it comes from her missing the other half of herself—her twin, Summer. While Summer has found her love and is trailing him around the world, Scarlet has been left alone for the first time in her life. She needs to find a husband who will treasure her, the way my Patrick treasures me.

But Scarlet hasn't had many dates that my dear Patrick approves of. How those two butt heads! It's as if Patrick sees himself in his headstrong young granddaughter.

I pray the man Scarlet chooses will be up to the test—and up to Patrick's standards. After all, there's nothing more important than family....

Dear Reader,

This April, leave the showers behind and embrace the warmth found only in a Silhouette Desire novel. First off is Susan Crosby's *The Forbidden Twin,* the latest installment in the scintillating continuity THE ELLIOTTS. This time, bad girl twin Scarlet sets her heart on seducing the one man she can't have. And speaking of wanting what you can't have, Peggy Moreland's *The Texan's Forbidden Affair* begins a brand-new series for this *USA TODAY* bestselling author. A PIECE OF TEXAS introduces a fabulous Lone Star legacy and stories that will stay with you long after the book is done.

Also launching this month is Maureen Child's SUMMER OF SECRETS, a trilogy about three handsome-as-sin cousins who are in for a season of scandalous revelations...and it all starts with *Expecting Lonergan's Baby.* Katherine Garbera wraps up her WHAT HAPPENS IN VEGAS...series with *Their Million-Dollar Night.* What woman could resist a millionaire who doesn't care about her past as long as she's willing to share his bed?

Making her Silhouette Desire debut this month is Silhouette Intimate Moments and HQN Books author Catherine Mann, with *Baby, I'm Yours.* Her delectable hero is certainly one guy this heroine should think about saying "I do" to once that pregnancy test comes back positive. And rounding out the month with a story of long-denied passion and shocking secrets is Anne Marie Winston's *The Soldier's Seduction.*

Enjoy all we have to offer this month!

Melissa Jeglinski

Melissa Jeglinski
Senior Editor
Silhouette Desire

Please address questions and book requests to:
Silhouette Reader Service
U.S.: 3010 Walden Ave., P.O. Box 1325, Buffalo, NY 14269
Canadian: P.O. Box 609, Fort Erie, Ont. L2A 5X3

SUSAN CROSBY

The Forbidden Twin

Silhouette *Desire*

Published by Silhouette Books

America's Publisher of Contemporary Romance

For Mabel, a woman of grace and humor.
Mom knew best.

Acknowledgment:
Special thanks and acknowledgment are
given to Susan Crosby for her contribution
to THE ELLIOTTS miniseries.

 SILHOUETTE BOOKS

ISBN 0-373-76717-X

THE FORBIDDEN TWIN

Visit Silhouette Books at www.eHarlequin.com

Printed in U.S.A.

Books by Susan Crosby

Silhouette Desire

The Mating Game #888
Almost a Honeymoon #952
Baby Fever #1018
Wedding Fever #1061
Marriage on His Mind #1108
Bride Candidate #9 #1131
*His Most Scandalous Secret #1158
*His Seductive Revenge #1162
*His Ultimate Temptation #1186
The Groom's Revenge #1214
The Baby Gift #1301
†Christmas Bonus, Strings Attached #1554
†Private Indiscretions #1570
†Hot Contact #1590
†Rules of Attraction #1647
†Heart of the Raven #1653
†Secrets of Paternity #1659
The Forbidden Twin #1717

*The Lone Wolves
†Behind Closed Doors

SUSAN CROSBY

believes in the value of setting goals, but also in the magic of making wishes. A longtime reader of romance novels, Susan earned a B.A. in English while raising her sons. She lives in the central valley of California, the land of wine grapes, asparagus and almonds. Her checkered past includes jobs as a synchronized swimming instructor, personnel interviewer at a toy factory and trucking company manager, but her current occupation as a writer is her all-time favorite.

Susan enjoys writing about people who take a chance on love, sometimes against all odds. She loves warm, strong heroes; good-hearted, self-reliant heroines…and happy endings.

Susan loves to hear from readers. You can visit her at her Web site, www.susancrosby.com.

THE ELLIOTTS

Patrick m Maeve O'Grady

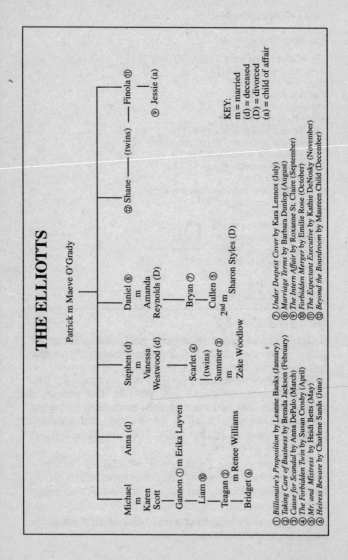

① *Billionaire's Proposition* by Leanne Banks (January)
② *Taking Care of Business* by Brenda Jackson (February)
③ *Cause for Scandal* by Anna DePalo (March)
④ *The Forbidden Twin* by Susan Crosby (April)
⑤ *Mr. and Mistress* by Heidi Betts (May)
⑥ *Heiress Beware* by Charlene Sands (June)
⑦ *Under Deepest Cover* by Kara Lennox (July)
⑧ *Marriage Terms* by Barbara Dunlop (August)
⑨ *The Intern Affair* by Roxanne St. Claire (September)
⑩ *Forbidden Merger* by Emilie Rose (October)
⑪ *The Expectant Executive* by Kathie DeNosky (November)
⑫ *Beyond the Boardroom* by Maureen Child (December)

KEY:
m = married
(d) = deceased
(D) = divorced
(a) = child of affair

One

Early March

John Harlan clutched a two-carat, brilliant-cut diamond engagement ring in one hand and a Glenfiddich on the rocks in the other, his third in the past hour. Cold had settled in his bones, his heart, his soul. It probably didn't help that he hadn't turned on the heat or even a lamp since night fell hours ago. Only the lights of New York City through his huge picture window illuminated his living room, making a hazy silhouette of the bottle of scotch on the coffee table. What more did he need to see than that, anyway?

A few hours ago his fiancée—former fiancée—had gently placed the diamond ring in his palm. He hadn't let go since.

John had thought he knew and understood Summer Elliott. She was goal-oriented and orderly, like him, and together they were dynamic, a power couple with great lineage and an amazing future. At twenty-nine, he was at a perfect age for marriage, and at a perfect point in his career at his advertising agency. Everything according to schedule.

She'd ended all possibility of a future together that afternoon.

He hadn't seen it coming.

They'd dated for months, long enough to know the relationship worked. They'd gotten engaged less than three weeks ago, on Valentine's Day, appropriately, romantically. And now, while he'd been in Chicago working with a new client this past week, she'd found herself another man—a rock star, of all people. Calm, sedate Summer Elliott, the woman whose personality matched his, had found herself a rock star.

John downed his scotch, relished the burn and was contemplating another when the doorbell rang. He didn't move. The bell rang again. He picked up the bottle and poured, the ice from the previous drink almost melted. Knuckles rapped on the door, and a female voice called his name.

Summer? No. She wouldn't come here.

Curious, however, he set the glass on the table and stood, taking a moment to shove his fingers through his hair and to find his balance. Although it was uncharacteristic of him to have more than a glass or two of wine in an evening, he wasn't drunk. At least he didn't think so, maybe just slightly off-kilter.

He opened his door and did a double take at the sight

of Summer standing at the elevator ten feet away, her back to him.

"What are you doing?" he asked, squinting against the light and stepping into the hall just as the elevator pinged, indicating its arrival on the fifteenth floor, his floor.

She spun to face him but said nothing. He registered that she looked different in her short red dress, but couldn't put his finger on exactly why. Her scintillating light auburn air caught the light, the soft, natural curl caressing her shoulders and drifting down her back. Her light green eyes were focused directly on him, her expression open and caring. Caring? Why should she care? She'd dumped him. Unceremoniously. Emotionlessly.

Which pretty much defined their relationship. Emotionless. Sexless. A partnership with a future based on a solid friendship and healthy respect for each other, if without passion. But he'd loved her and believed she'd loved him. He'd always figured the passion part would fall into place at some point, and had respected her wishes to save herself for the marriage bed.

Had she realized her mistake in breaking it off with him? Was that why she was here?

Why wasn't she talking? She'd come to see him, after all.

"Are you here to apologize?" he asked. Did he *want* her to apologize?

"Made a mistake," she said so low he could barely hear her. She walked toward him, her hand outstretched. "A big mistake." Her fingertips grazed his chest, then she pulled back as if burned, curling her fingers into a fist that she pressed against her heart.

His gut tightened. Her touch had been light, but lethal

to his equilibrium. Hope tried to shove hours of hurt out of the way. The hurt resisted giving way...until she reached out again and was suddenly kissing him—kissing the hell out of him. Caught off guard by her new, surreal level of passion, he kissed her back until she moaned, even as a cautionary voice in his head shouted at him not to forgive the woman who'd never slept with *him,* her fiancé, yet who'd given herself to a man she'd just met.

When she pressed her hips to his and moved against him, he was grateful he hadn't had that fourth drink and could still think clearly enough to know what to do next. Resisting wasn't an option, even though he'd spent months doing exactly that. Not this time, however. Not this time.

He scooped her into his arms, carried her to his bed and laid her on the comforter, deciding that the reason she looked different was that she'd come dressed to seduce him—something she'd never done before.

An unexpected warmth spread through him at the thought that she'd made that kind of effort for him.

"This is out of the blue," he said, turning the words into a question, wanting to trust her motives, but afraid to. What did it say about him if he so easily forgave her?

"I never expected to make love with you."

He frowned. "What do you mean?"

"Just that."

It wasn't an answer, but apparently it was all he was going to get. Had the bad-boy rock star already dumped her? Did it matter? Yes. But...*but* John wanted to show her what she'd been missing as he'd reined himself in all those months, honoring her self-imposed pledge of chastity. His ego even demanded it.

He turned on a bedside lamp, pulled off his tie and un-buttoned his shirt, his movements jerky. She wasn't telling him to stop. She was really going through with it?

He shrugged off his shirt and tossed it aside, reached for his belt buckle and pulled his belt out of the loops, letting it drop to the floor, noticing her spiky red high heels there, as well, a vivid reminder of the strangeness of the evening. He'd never seen her wear heels that high, which put her equal in height to him.

Equal. Was that the point? To make them equals? She'd suddenly become aggressive, not merely assertive?

His jaw tightened painfully as he searched her face, seeking answers to questions he didn't ask because he wasn't sure he wanted the answers. Not only did she not tell him to stop, she didn't even flinch and instead studied his every move, not a hint of virginal shyness in her eyes. He toed off his shoes, slipped his trousers down and off, along with his socks.

His briefs were black and tight, had gone tighter in the past few minutes. She made a leisurely inspection of him that was more exciting than any kiss or touch he could remember. She swallowed and lifted her eyes to meet his again. Her nipples pressed against her dress. His heart thundered; his fists clenched.

If he took off the briefs, would she run? She'd kept him at arm's length for months and months, yet after she'd slept with another man, she wanted *him* now? What kind of sense did that make? Comparison? It was totally out of character for her.

And if he slept with her now, would it be in forgiveness…or out of revenge? He wasn't sure if he even wanted to find out, but an irrational force made him continue, even knowing he might be shot down or stopped. Or humiliated.

Except she'd said she'd made a mistake....

He pushed off the briefs. She rose to her knees and reached out to touch him, her fingertips gliding down him like warm, silky water. He sucked in a breath, knelt on the bed and peeled her formfitting dress over her head, discovering a red lacy bra and matching thong underneath. He pushed the satin straps down her arms, the weight of her breasts taking the fabric temptingly lower, the lace hanging up on her nipples. Her lemony scent drifted up to him.

His mouth went dry. He'd imagined Summer as a white-bra-and-panties woman....

He lifted his gaze to hers as he laid his palms on her breasts, feeling the smooth, warm firmness of her flesh, the heels of his hands grazing her hard nipples. She was so different from what he'd expected. So sexy. So willing. So...

So not Summer.

"Scarlet?" he managed to ask, taking his hands away, sure of her identity even as he asked the question. No wonder she was different. Not Summer, but her identical twin sister. Scarlet had a wild reputation, but he never would've guessed she would pretend to be her sister. What purpose did it serve? She'd always been standoffish with him, as if she didn't like him.

She sat back, confusion in her eyes. "Have you ever seen Summer wear a dress like that?"

He could tell her he was three-quarters drunk, but it would seem like an insult. "I thought she'd come to seduce me."

Scarlet's lack of answer could mean anything. He wouldn't try to second-guess her.

Mistaken identities aside, he was acutely aware that his arousal hadn't suffered at the recognition of Summer's twin. If anything, the shock of the revelation excited him even more, though he didn't stop to determine why—didn't want to determine why, except he'd endured a long abstinence.

"What are you doing here?" he asked, tired of waiting, frustrated by her actions and his own wayward thoughts.

She rose to her knees again and set her hands on his chest. For several endless seconds their gazes locked. "Does it matter?"

Not at the moment, but soon it would probably matter a lot. Her words about never expecting to make love with him echoed in his head. "You hadn't intended to make love? Then what—"

"Maybe you shouldn't be thinking so hard," she said, drawing him closer.

Her touch erased all thoughts, banished all doubts, and he let go of his curiosity and kissed her instead. He forgot about Summer and opened himself up to Scarlet….

Scarlet, who made incredibly sexy, needy sounds that vibrated from her throat, whose hands wandered over his body as he sought her in the same way. He flicked open her bra, tossed it aside, captured a nipple between his lips, then tongued the hard contours before drawing it into his mouth and savoring as she arched her back, her fingernails digging into him to keep her balance. He took as much care with her other breast, but need pounded him relentlessly, especially when she wrapped her hand around him as he throbbed and ached.

He jerked back, trying to slow down. This was probably the stupidest thing he'd done in his life, but he couldn't stop— Yes, he could. He just didn't want to.

He set his hands on her waist to help her stand, then he eased her thong down her legs. Grasping his head, she leaned over to kiss him, kissed him as he'd never been kissed before, with lips and teeth and tongue, until he couldn't wait another second. He shoved her onto her back and moved her thighs apart. He watched as he entered her, clenched his teeth at the hot tightness that enveloped him, felt her contract, heard her long, low moan that quickly escalated in volume and tempo. He squeezed his eyes shut, holding back, waiting for her, then he exploded inside her. Sensation bombarded him, starting deep and low then racing through his body, even into his mind, blocking everything but feeling, hot, overwhelming feeling. It was good. She was good. Incredible....

He resisted the return of logic and sanity, which came regardless of his wishes. He rolled onto his back and stared at the ceiling. She lay silent beside him. Silent and still. He couldn't even hear her breathe. Her perfume mingled with the earthy smell of sex. He wouldn't soon forget it.

He would *never* forget it.

He turned toward her—

The mattress jiggled as she rolled away from him and off the bed. She gathered up her clothes and hurried to his bathroom, shutting the door.

Shutting him out.

Scarlet tried to let her mind go blank as she dressed inside John's elegant bathroom. She focused on the black fixtures and brushed-nickel faucets. She avoided the mirror as long as she could, then she had to look.

Mascara smudges under her eyes made her skin look paler and her eyes darker than usual. She dampened a tissue and cleaned off the smudges, then finger-combed her hair, stalling, not wanting to face him again.

What had she done?

She'd only come to tell him she thought Summer had made a huge mistake in ending their engagement. Then somehow they were kissing. Scarlet had told him the truth. She'd never expected to kiss him—ever—much less make love with him. She may have cultivated a reputation for outrageousness in the past, but this was over the top, even for her.

The problem was, Scarlet had been in love with John forever, feelings she'd had to keep to herself when she realized he and Summer had discovered an affinity for each other—then they'd realized they were in love just about the time when Scarlet was going to tell Summer how she felt about John herself.

Scarlet had envied the way John had treated Summer, the way he looked into her eyes when she talked, the way he touched her whenever he was near, a sweep of a hand down her back or the surprisingly sexy brush of her curls with his fingers. But it was his consideration of Summer that had made Scarlet the most envious— how much time he spent with her. How they never seemed to run out of things to say, their discussions deep and long. How he always called to say good-night and good-morning.

Scarlet had never had a man treat her like that.

Well, consider the source.

She closed her eyes for a moment, not wanting to dwell on her own shortcomings.

She'd ignored those tender feelings she'd had for John for a long time, had avoided ever having a private discussion with him, fearing he might see how she felt. She'd thought she had those feelings well under control, had made herself stop thinking about him in a romantic light when her sister had gotten serious with him, but seeing him tonight, seeing his pain, had made her realize she hadn't stopped caring, that she'd only shoved everything aside because of Summer.

And now Scarlet needed to kill those feelings once and for all. She and John couldn't have a relationship. Propriety would be reason enough, never mind that he wouldn't want to have anything to do with her beyond this night, since it would keep him in proximity with Summer, as well. This was a once-in-a-lifetime opportunity. Over and done. Relegated to the memory book.

She brushed her hands down her dress then opened the bathroom door. He was still lying in bed, his hands tucked under his head, the sheet pulled up to his waist.

She hunted down her shoes, put them on, wobbling some because she was shaking.

He threw back the covers, climbed out of bed and set his hands on her shoulders. "Take it easy, okay? Nothing—"

"You could at least cover up," she said, wincing at her snippy tone.

After a moment he grinned, revealing heart-tugging dimples. She stopped a sigh from escaping. He was one fine-looking man, with those intense dark brown eyes and sandy brown hair. Who would've guessed that hidden under his boring business suits was such a remarkable body, strong, muscular and toned. Tempting.

"You're leaving, I guess," he said.

"Of course I'm leaving. Do you think I'm an idiot?" She closed her eyes. "Scratch that question." Her behavior already gave her idiocy away.

He looked at her curiously, then grabbed his briefs and donned them. "Why did this happen, Scarlet?"

She searched for a reason he would believe. The only thing that came to mind was what Summer had confided earlier that day when she'd told Scarlet that she was ending her engagement with John—that even though she'd loved him, there had been a complete lack of chemistry between them. For months she'd thought she was just sublimating her passion, so that she could avoid sleeping with him until their wedding night. One hour with rock star Zeke Woodlow had changed all that.

But Scarlet couldn't believe that Summer had been talking about the same man who'd just made love to *her*. Lack of chemistry? Not a chance. The man Scarlet had just made love to took passion to a whole new level.

"Cat got your tongue?" John asked.

All she could do was give him a weak smile.

"Why did this happen?" he repeated.

"Because we got carried away?"

"I know why I would, but why would you?"

She couldn't tell him she loved him, so what could she say? After a few seconds, she felt him touch her cheek. The tenderness of the gesture almost made her throw herself into his arms.

"I figure you know I never slept with your sister."

She nodded. "She was wrong, though. You are a passionate man."

His mouth quirked. "Maybe it's just you. Maybe you brought that out in me." He brushed her hair behind an ear, then rubbed her earlobe. "How about helping me hone my skills? I never want to disappoint another woman."

"This is no time to joke. You don't need lessons, and we have no future together. What happened shouldn't have happened, and I'm sorry."

He narrowed his gaze. "Sorry? For what?"

"I know you must be hurt and angry, and you probably even want revenge, but please, please, don't tell anyone what happened," she said, then walked away before he could say or do anything to stop her. She was confused, not sure why she had done what she'd done, or what she could do about it now. She needed to get away and think. She grabbed her purse off the living-room floor and raced out the door, then hurried down a flight of stairs just to get away fast. She picked up the elevator on the next floor.

The doorman called good-night as she left the building. She stepped into the cold, damp evening and realized she'd forgotten her coat. She couldn't go back for it.

She couldn't go home, either, to her grandparents' town house where she and Summer shared the top floor. Summer probably wasn't even home, might even be with Zeke, but Scarlet didn't want to take the chance. She would get a hotel room for the night, order a bottle of wine, take a hot bath and figure out where she'd gone wrong.

Except that it hadn't felt wrong—not when she was in John's arms. It had felt so…right. He wasn't her sister's fiancé anymore. She hadn't violated any codes of ethics, sibling or otherwise. She and Summer had made a pact when they were eight years old that they would never pretend to be the other, and while she'd gone to John's apartment as herself, she knew fairly soon that he'd thought she was her sister and she hadn't corrected his mistake until it was almost past the point of no return. If he hadn't realized it on his own, she would've told him, though—wouldn't she?

Yes, of course. Probably.

So…a bath, some wine and some reflection. She would put John Harlan out of her mind once and for all.

And by morning she would be fine.

Just fine.

Two

Early April

Scarlet glared at her watch. A quarter past noon. She checked her cell phone, making sure it was turned on. It was. No missed calls. No voice-mail messages. Irritation whipped through her. It was unlike Summer to keep her waiting, especially for fifteen minutes. But then, Summer had lost her predictability. She'd even gotten herself engaged to Zeke Woodlow less than a month after ending her engagement to—

Scarlet went no further with the thought. At least there was a sparkle in Summer's eyes and a lightness in her step that hadn't been there before. A totally different kind of aura surrounded her, and for that Scarlet thanked Zeke.

He'd just better not ever hurt her....

Pasting on a smile, Scarlet returned a wave to a fellow employee then stabbed a piece of avocado in her Cobb salad. Seated in the company cafeteria, she was grateful she'd been able to grab a booth. She hated eating alone in public—Summer knew that. And it was especially bad here where noise bounced off the walls and the steel tabletops, the modern decor not helping to absorb sound, not letting a person think clearly. Plus, the entire twenty-five-story Park Avenue building was owned by EPH—Elliott Publication Holdings, her family's business. Or rather, businesses, their many magazines, so that a lot of people could pick her out of a crowd. Plus she was an Elliott, one who'd already caused enough talk.

She should've told Summer to meet her at the deli down the block.

"Who are you waiting for?"

Scarlet looked up to find Finola Elliott, editor in chief of *Charisma* magazine and Scarlet's boss for the past two years—and for twenty-five years, her aunt Finny.

"Summer. She's late."

"That's unlike her."

"I know."

Fin lowered her voice. "Are you okay?"

Surprised, Scarlet focused on her aunt instead of the cafeteria entrance. "Sure. Why?"

"You've seemed tense lately."

"I'm fine," she said, resisting the temptation to make a similar comment to Fin, who was under a great deal of stress since her father, Scarlet's grandfather, had issued a challenge regarding who was to fill his shoes when he retired at the end of the year—a challenge which had only added to the long-standing tension existing between Fin and her parents. The fact that Fin was eating in the company cafeteria instead of the executive dining room indicated her discomfort, as well.

"I'd ask you to join us, Fin, but Summer called this meeting. Here she is now."

"No problem," Fin said as Summer hugged her then slipped into the booth. "I'm meeting Bridget. See you later."

"Sorry I'm late," Summer said, her eyes shimmering. "Cute outfit. Can I borrow it?"

Scarlet smiled. Even though Summer had made sweeping changes recently, her wardrobe still wouldn't include anything like the purple-and-red minidress that Scarlet had designed and made this past week. "My closet is your closet," Scarlet said.

Summer laughed.

Scarlet could usually anticipate what her sister would say, but not this time. Not for the past few weeks, actually. She only knew that Summer was revved about something. "What's up?"

She linked her fingers together and set her hands on the table. "I'm taking a leave of absence from *The Buzz*."

Shock heated Scarlet from the inside out. "Why?"

"I want to go with Zeke on his international tour."

"For how long?"

"A month."

Scarlet could barely find words. "We've never been apart for more than a week."

"Life is changing, Scar. *We're* changing."

"Separating." *I used to be able to read your mind. We used to finish each other's sentences.*

"It was bound to happen someday." Understanding *and* determination rang in Summer's voice.

"I can't believe you're giving up your dream job, and an imminent promotion, for a…man."

"Not just any man, but Zeke. The man I love." Her calm voice was offset by a stubborn glint in her eye. "The man I'm going to marry."

"When do you leave?"

"Tomorrow."

"So soon?" Scarlet felt more vulnerable than ever. Her link to life as she knew it was breaking. It had been hard enough this past month not to confide in Summer about her night with John Harlan, especially when Summer had asked her where she'd been all night.

"Don't be jealous," Summer said, laying her hand on Scarlet's.

"Jealous? I—" She stopped. Maybe she was, a little. She'd been wanting to try her hand at fashion design but hadn't had the nerve to quit her job as assistant fashion editor for *Charisma*. "Granddad will accuse you of being ungrateful," she said to her sister instead, reminding herself of that fact, as well—the main reason why she hadn't quit her job herself.

"That's what I'm afraid of. But Zeke has tried to convince me otherwise. Loyalty matters more than anything to Granddad, but I need to do this. I want to do this. I'm *going* to do this."

And everyone thought Summer was the meek twin. "Have you told him?"

"I'm telling you first. I'll tell Shane after lunch. Then Gram and Granddad."

Shane—Uncle Shane—was Fin's twin and the editor

in chief of *The Buzz,* EPH's showbiz magazine, where Summer worked as a copy editor, and was about to be promoted to reporter. Scarlet didn't envy Summer telling Shane or, worse, Granddad.

"I'm going to miss you like crazy," Scarlet said, nearly crushing Summer's hand.

"Me, too," she whispered, her eyes instantly bright. "I'll call lots. I promise. Maybe you could meet us somewhere on the tour for a weekend."

"Three's a crowd." Scarlet made an effort to keep things as normal as possible. She dug into her salad again. "Want some?"

"Butterflies," Summer said, patting her stomach.

Scarlet nodded. "What I said about my closet being your closet is true, you know. If you'd like to take some of my stuff on the tour, you can."

"Zeke likes me as I am."

So had John, Scarlet thought. Summer was so much easier to be with—not anywhere near as demanding of equality or independence as Scarlet. At least, not openly.

"There you go again," Summer said, tapping the table next to Scarlet's salad bowl.

"What?"

"You've been zoning out for, I don't know, about a month now."

"Have I?"

"Yes. Right after you spent the night away from home and wouldn't tell me where you'd been. Seems to me you've been keeping a secret, and that's a first for us, too."

Scarlet wanted so much to talk to Summer about John, about that night, but that was impossible. There was no one she could talk to, except the man himself, maybe, but he hadn't contacted her at all, and she both resented and appreciated his self-control. Except for having her coat delivered to her office the next day, without a note, they hadn't existed for each other.

Except that her body hungered in a way it never had.

"Can we spend the evening together?" Scarlet asked, changing the subject altogether, then noting the hurt in her sister's eyes. But Scarlet couldn't confide. Nothing would ever change that. Some secrets would be taken to the grave.

"You'll help me pack?"

"Sure."

"I don't know what time I'll be home. I'm taking the helicopter to The Tides to tell the Grands."

"I'll wait up. We'll have margaritas. You'll need one." Scarlet added teasingly, "Better you than me this time."

Summer grinned. "I know. The shoe's finally on the other foot. For years you've made it your goal to irritate Granddad with your men of choice, and I've always tried to get you to stop doing that. The Grands have taken their role as guardians seriously since Mom and Dad died. I guess after fifteen years in that role it's hard to change. And of course, Granddad still cares about image."

"He cares too much about image." And Scarlet thought, they hadn't really been her "men of choice," but men she'd chosen specifically to irritate her over-bearing grandfather. Men came and went. Very few had been lovers. Most were just friends.

Then there was John. She missed him. How had that happened? But she couldn't reach out to him—she, who'd never been known for her patience, had con-trolled her impulse to contact him, made easier by the fact that he'd left town, or so the rumor went. In mourning for losing Summer?

"I need to get going," Summer said. "I'll call you when I'm headed home, as long as Granddad lets me take the copter back. If not, it's a long ride from the Hamptons."

"I'll go up the elevator with you," Scarlet said, not wanting to stay in the booth alone.

They waited at the doors. Scarlet would get off at the seventeenth floor, Summer one higher.

Scarlet swept her into a big hug as the elevator rose with silent speed. "Promise you won't change."

"Can't."

Scarlet pulled back and brushed her sister's hair from her face. "Is it wonderful, being in love?"

"Zeke is an amazing man."

The simple statement, layered with tenderness, almost made Scarlet cry. She wanted that for herself—a partner, an amazing partner. One who cared for her more than anyone, who thought *she* was amazing. Someone who was hers, and hers alone, as she would be his alone.

"I love you," Scarlet said as the elevator door opened.

"Me, too, you."

Scarlet stepped out of the elevator and headed for her cubicle, past the dazzling sign with the company slogan—*Charisma, Fashion for the Body*. The bright turquoise color scheme and edgy, bold patterns seemed to shout at her. Everything was topsy-turvy. She needed a little peace.

She would find none in her cubicle, which was filled with photos and swatches and drawings—colorful and eye-catching, not soothing. She grabbed her sketch pad and flipped to a blank page. She drew almost without thought—a wedding gown for Summer, with a long veil and train, something fairy-tale princesslike, a fantasy dress, layered with organza, scattered with a few pearls and crystals, but nothing flashy, just enough to catch the light. Elegant, like Summer.

Scarlet turned the page and sketched another wedding dress—strapless, formfitting, no train, no veil, just a few flowers threaded in the bride's long, light auburn hair—hers.

She stared at it, her pencil poised over the pad, then tore off the page, crumpled it into a ball and tossed it in the trash can. Turning to her computer, she opened a work file. She wasn't the Cinderella type. She would skip the grand ceremony, the stress of the spectacle and have something simple instead, if she ever married. Married was married. It didn't matter how it happened.

Her phone rang. Her one o'clock appointment had arrived. She stood, hesitated, then pulled the wadded-up design from her trash can. Her hands shaking slightly, she smoothed out the wrinkles and tucked it back into the pad behind Summer's design.

It was a good design, she thought, something she should redo and put in her portfolio—that was the reason she'd retrieved it. She didn't throw away good work.

Liar. The word bounced in her head, as much in accusation as relief, but above all, honest, a trait that seemed in short supply these days.

Three

At 9:00 p.m., two days later, John stood in front of the Elliott town house near 90th and Amsterdam. The gray stone building sported stately white trim and a playful red front door. He put his hand on the ivy-covered, black wrought-iron gate meant to keep out passersby. He knew of another entrance, however, a private entrance that would take him to the third, and top, floor—Summer and Scarlet's living quarters, comprised of a bedroom suite for each and a communal living room.

The home's owners, Patrick and Maeve Elliott, patriarch and matriarch of the Elliott clan, spent most of their time these days at The Tides, their estate in the Hamptons. Summer and Scarlet were raised there by their grandparents after their parents' deaths in a plane crash. Now the girls lived mostly in the city, occasionally going home to The Tides on weekends.

John's family owned an estate neighboring the Elliotts' in the Hamptons, yet they'd had little contact through the years. John was four years older than the twins. He'd headed to college when they were just entering high school. A couple of years after Summer and Scarlet graduated from college, he'd met them as adults and became an occasional companion to Summer, their relationship escalating from there. No big romance, just an increasing presence and steadily growing relationship.

This last month away from New York had given him perspective. He and Summer had never been suited for each other. They were too much alike, both with their five-year plans, career focuses and even-keeled personalities.

She'd changed, apparently. He'd read in some Hollywood gossip column that she'd accompanied Zeke Woodlow on tour to Europe. Amazing. Who would've guessed that such an adventurous spirit lived inside her?

Over and done, he reminded himself. Now he needed to see Scarlet. The month's separation had allowed him to acknowledge the absurdity of anything happening beyond their one stolen night, but he knew they would run into each other now and then, so they needed to settle things between them.

He hadn't called her, although many times he'd picked up to the phone to do so. Nor had she called him. And as bold and direct as she was, the fact that she hadn't made contact spoke volumes. It had been a one-night stand for both of them.

He reached for his cell phone to alert her he was there, then didn't make the call. He knew he should—

it was unlike him not to be courteous. He had no idea
if she was even at home, or alone, but he wanted to catch
her off guard and see her real reaction to him, not something manufactured while waiting for him to climb the
stairs, so he punched in the security code to enter the
half-underground four-car garage, slipped inside the
door and strode past the indoor pool and up the staircase to Scarlet's floor.

Nerves played havoc with his equilibrium. The
thought caught him by surprise, keeping him from
ringing her bell immediately. Maybe he should've worn
a suit, shown her—and himself—that he meant business. Instead he'd pulled on a sweater, khakis and
loafers, as casual as he owned. At the last minute he'd
slapped on some aftershave, something with a citrus
base that reminded him of Scarlet's perfume, which had
lingered on his skin for days, it seemed, showers not
ridding his memory of the fragrance. He'd gotten hard
every night in bed just thinking about it, about her, about
the way she'd admired and touched him, about the way
she kissed, and moved, and—

Hell, things were stirring *now.*

He rang the bell, needing to get the conversation
over with so that he could move on with his life. After
a few seconds, a shadow darkened the peephole, then
came a few long, dragged-out seconds of anticipation.
Maybe she wouldn't even open the door, or acknowledge she was home....

The doorknob turned; the door opened slowly.

The living room lights were off. Behind her the open
door to her bedroom spilled enough light to cast her in silhouette. He saw only her outline, her hair around her

shoulders, a floor-length robe. Her perfume reached his nose, drifted through him, arousing him the rest of the way.

"John?"

How he'd ever confused her voice with her sister's the other time was beyond him. Scarlet's was silky, sultry…sexy.

"Are you alone, Scarlet?"

"Yes." She gestured toward the living room. "Come in."

He looked around, as if seeing it for the first time. He'd been there often with Summer, yet everything seemed different. He saw Scarlet's modern influence now instead of Summer's more homey leanings, the eclectic mix of antiques and minimalist furnishings effective and dramatic.

"Have a seat," she said, indicating the couch in front of the picture window overlooking the street. She pulled her robe around her a little more, tightened the sash, switched on a lamp, then sat at the opposite end of the couch.

Her breasts were unrestrained; her nipples jutted against the fabric. He could hardly keep his eyes off her. He knew she was waiting for him to start the conversation, to let her know why he'd come. He wasn't sure of his reasons anymore.

"How have you been?" he asked finally, starting slowly, gauging her reaction to him being there without an invitation.

"Fine. And you?"

"Okay." *Inane. Say something important, something honest.*

She smoothed the fabric along her thighs. He wanted to do that, too, then lay his head in her lap.

"Where did you go?" she asked.

"L.A. My partners and I are expanding the markets for some new clients, growing the firm. It seemed like a good time to go."

"So your decision was because of business, not because of—"

She didn't finish the sentence. Would she have said "Summer" or herself?

She angled toward him a little, which created a gap in the robe, allowing him a glimpse of the upper swell of her lush breast. He really needed to stop fixating on her body.

"Business," he said. Which was not entirely true. He'd manufactured some business that needed one of the partners' attention, then had volunteered to go. His ad agency was already hugely successful, but there was always room to expand.

"I see."

A long silence followed.

"Why are you here, John?"

He finally remembered the reason. "I just wanted to make sure you were okay with…what happened. I don't want things to be awkward between us, since we're bound to run into each other now and then."

"I think picturing you naked will remove any sense of awkwardness for me."

Her eyes took on some sparkle. He was glad to see it.

"It's vivid for me, too," he said.

"It was good, John, but emotionally charged. We need to remember that. Make it real, instead of…"

"Surreal."

"Exactly. A fantasy, nothing more."

"And a one-time thing." He added the tiniest inflection at the end, turning the phrase into a question if she chose to hear it that way.

"Absolutely." Definite. Certain. No question.

He looked away. He had his answer. "Okay. I'm glad we cleared that up."

"Me, too."

He shifted a little. "I didn't use protection."

"We both got carried away. But there's no problem."

"Good. Great." He stood. "I'll go, then."

He heard her follow him. The air seemed thick. Breathing took effort. He turned when he reached the door, wishing he could read her mind.

"Is there something else you want?" she asked, reaching toward him then pulling back.

"You," he answered, catching her hand, tugging her toward him. "I want you."

"John…." There was hunger in her voice, need in her eyes.

Then they were in each other's arms, kissing, moaning, hands wandering, bodies pressing. She tipped her head back as he dragged his mouth down her neck, her robe separating, revealing her naked body, warm and dewy, as if she'd just stepped out of the bath.

"You're all I've thought about," he said just before drawing a nipple into his mouth, cupping the most feminine part of her with his hand. "You. This."

"Me, too." Her voice was deep, breathy. "Come with me."

He went willingly into her bedroom. Lights were on full. Sketches were everywhere—tacked on corkboard on the wall, scattered over the floor, even on the bed, an unmade jumble of linens. She swept the papers away.

They drifted to the floor, as did her pale blue robe, pooling around her feet, making her look like a goddess rising from the sea.

He jerked his sweater over his head, got rid of his shoes and socks. He touched his belt. She brushed his hands away and undid it, all the while looking at his face. Her color was high, her cheekbones sharp, her eyes a deeper green. Her lips were swollen from kissing, and parted slightly. He felt his slacks drop to the floor and kicked them away. Then she hooked his briefs and tugged. As she knelt to remove them, her hair brushed his abdomen, then his thighs, his shins.

He dug his fingers into her scalp, pulled her hair into his fists, squeezed his eyes shut. A month of fantasies became reality. Hell, not just a month, a lifetime, but a month of specific fantasies about one particular woman.

When her exploration became more daring, he pulled her up, moved her back and made her stretch out on the bed. He wanted to drag it out, make it last, but he lost all sense of control and finesse. He plunged into her. She arched into him. His body blasted apart in a long series of hot, explosive, rhythmic sensations. She clenched him from inside and climaxed with him, her face contorted, her mouth open. Then their movements slowed…stopped. He rolled over, taking her along. She stretched out on top of him and he wrapped her close.

For a long time, neither spoke.

Scarlet had spent the better part of the past month—months, really—convincing herself that she didn't love John, that she'd merely been infatuated because he was so different, attentive to Summer in ways that no man had been attentive to her. She'd been envious, that was all, and had created a fantasy about him. Now she was back at square one. Because she did love him.

Now, how could she keep him in her life long enough for those feelings to run their course? Obviously absence hadn't helped. And obviously they couldn't go public. People would assume that John and Summer had slept together, so the idea of Scarlet sleeping with her sister's ex-fiancé was— She couldn't even come up with the right words.

Appearances were important, especially for John, personally and professionally. And while Scarlet had a reputation, such a liaison with John would be beyond her usual outrageousness. How could they get past that? Not to mention him coming in contact with Summer.

And also not to mention she was probably a kind of substitute for her sister, a way to end his curiosity about her. Why else would he have come on this strong? He would certainly want closure; *she* would, in his shoes. Since he'd missed out on a physical relationship with Summer, having one with Scarlet *could* give him closure. Of sorts.

The thought that she and Summer might be interchangeable in his mind made her a little sick to her stomach. But maybe he wasn't thinking that way at all. Maybe she was just imagining it.

So, now what? It seemed to Scarlet they needed to let the attraction burn in a controlled environment or it might be a bank of embers forever, taking on too much importance as time passed, always waiting to flare.

She had an idea….

"Do you still want lessons?" she asked, burrowing against him, not wanting to see his face.

His arms tightened around her, and he drew a long breath, as if she'd awakened him. "Lessons?"

"Last time you asked for help honing your skills."

"You said I didn't need lessons."

"Not in bed. But you could learn something about being more romantic if you want to woo a woman into bed…in the regular way."

After a long, drawn-out moment of silence, he rolled to his side with her, then propped himself on an elbow to look her in the eyes. His were filled with humor. His dimples deepened. "Woo?"

She shoved his shoulder as he laughed, apparently at her use of such an old-fashioned term. "You have to admit you could use lessons."

His smile faded some. "I admit it. Instinct doesn't seem to be serving me well. Except—" he slid a hand down her back and pulled her closer "—where you're concerned."

"Only in regards to sex, then." She knew he didn't return her feelings.

"No stronger instinct, is there?"

She shrugged.

He stroked her hair, tucked it behind her ear. "So, you'd be willing to advise me on how to properly *woo* a woman? What would that entail?"

Lots of time together. Lots of touching. Lots of—
"Lessons," she said instead.

"Homework?"

She hadn't thought about that. He would have to experiment on other women, to see if the lessons worked.

That would never do. "You'll practice on me. If you can make *me* fall under your spell, then you know it can work on any woman."

"She says humbly."

"I'm not being egotistical. I'm just immune to the games of most men."

"What happens if you do fall under my spell?"

She had no answer for that. She'd dug a ditch she couldn't climb out of, however.

"Seems to me this is a game with potentially disastrous outcomes," he said.

"Or fun ones." She laid a hand along his face. "It's very selfish, I suppose, to want this."

"But if we're both in agreement, what's the harm?"

"We're adults, after all."

He said nothing for a few seconds, then seemed to relax. "When would we start?"

"Sometime when we're dressed."

He grinned. "In the meantime…" He hooked a leg over hers, bringing her closer then kissing her until she forgot everything but the feel of his mouth. "Will this be part of the wooing?" he asked, dragging his lips along her jaw.

Huh? Oh. He was talking to her.

She didn't answer immediately. She understood that he was trying to figure out what the parameters of their relationship were going to be. She wanted more than sex, but she knew that was all she could have. Too much stood in their way, especially how quickly they got together after the breakup. Should she settle for only sex? Would the desire fizzle in time?

"I'm enjoying this as much as you are," she said

truthfully, testing his own expectations. "Although we both know—"

He put a hand over her mouth. "We do. And we don't need to talk about it."

She moved his hand away. "I wouldn't have guessed that you were an avoider of truth."

"It's my superhero role. That's why you never see me in tights and a cape, and only in suits."

"Oh, *that's* why. I did wonder."

"When do we start Woo University? Tomorrow?"

So, they weren't going to define their relationship yet. Maybe that was a good thing for now. "Why wait?" she asked.

"I'm not done registering for class yet." He rolled on top of her, bent to kiss her. "Haven't finished uploading from my hard drive."

She laughed. Who would've thought the man could be so playful? "You're not what I expected."

"In what way?"

"In every way. You always seem so serious."

"You'd never seen me naked."

She smiled. "I guess it does make a difference."

He nuzzled her neck. "You're not what you seemed, either."

Her body tingled from the feel of his warm breath against her skin. "How?"

"Less bold."

"I thought I'd been plenty bold."

"Sexually, you have been."

"What other way is there?"

He didn't answer. The hand that had been roaming over her body stilled. "Do you really want to spend our time analyzing this?" he asked, pulling away, locking gazes.

No. It was a time to enjoy him, to make memories. He would change her life—she knew that without a doubt—but her obsession could finally end and she could move on, once and for all. Her relationship with her sister would never have to be tested, nor would Scarlet give the publicity hounds something to sniff out. If Summer could change, so could she.

"No," she said, looping her arms around his shoulders and pulling him down to kiss him. "No analysis necessary. Although I do plan to study your moves."

"As a mentor?"

She smiled slowly. "As a woman."

"Nothing like putting on the pressure."

His words may have indicated a lack of self-confidence but his actions didn't. He knew exactly what to touch, and how, and when. She couldn't remember being aroused so skillfully. But was that all there was—skill? Was his heart engaged even the slightest?

He cupped her face. She opened her eyes, sensing a question coming.

"You don't seem to be in the moment," he said.

"I am completely in the moment," she replied honestly, although his interpretation was probably different from her own. All her desires, all her fears raced through her mind. She wanted to ignore them. They refused to go away.

His silence lasted several long seconds. He started to pull away. She wrapped him close, drew him down… and gave him no more reason to wonder.

Four

John picked up his office telephone the next day, started to punch in a number, then stopped. His first homework assignment was to ask Scarlet for a date in the way he usually asked a woman out. He had to think about it. When he was seeing Summer they'd talked every day and decided together what they would do. He'd never *wooed* her, since they'd just sort of fallen into the relationship gradually. It had been a long time since he'd asked out a woman.

He ran a hand down his face, then dialed Scarlet's work number, feeling like a novice at this dating game instead of a twenty-nine-year-old veteran.

"Scarlet Elliott," she answered, all businesslike.

Which turned him on. He pictured her as she was last night, leaning against her headboard, her hair tangled, face flushed, the sheet tucked over her chest but drifting bit by bit while they talked, until he'd tugged it away and gathered her close.

"Hel-lo?" she singsonged.

He ignored his body's stirrings. "Good morning."

A pause, then, "Who's calling?"

"The man who heated up your sheets last night."

"Stop that," she said in almost a whisper. "You're supposed to have just met me and are asking for a date."

Role-playing? He considered that for a moment. It might be fun—for a day or so. "Not my fault. My mentor didn't give me a syllabus for my first Woo U class."

He heard her laugh briefly.

"Start over." She hung up before he had a chance to say a word.

John sat back in surprise then began to laugh. He redialed.

"Scarlet Elliott."

"Good morning, Ms. Elliott. This is John Harlan of Suskind, Engle and Harlan. We met at the *Charisma* open house over the holidays."

She sighed. "If you have to add the name of your firm, you didn't make much of an impression in the first place. Start over." She hung up.

He was tempted not to call her back, but after a minute, he did.

"Scarlet Elliott."

"Good morning, Ms. Elliott. This is John Harlan. We met at the *Charisma* open house over the holidays."

"I remember. You defended the existence of Santa Claus quite well."

He smiled. "Someone told me your name was Virginia."

"Friend or foe?" she asked.

"Someone who wanted me to embarrass myself, apparently, by calling you by the wrong name."

"You didn't. Embarrass yourself."

Was there double meaning in her remark? "That's good to hear." He was aware she wasn't calling him by name, probably so that no one could overhear her. "I'd like to get to know you better. I was wondering if you would have dinner with me."

"When?"

"Saturday night." This was too easy. How long could he draw out the lessons? He'd have to play dumb just to drag it out.

A long pause ensued. "This is Friday," she said coolly.

"Would you rather go out tonight?"

Dead silence.

He brushed a speck of dust from his slacks. Something told him he'd just messed up his first assignment, big-time. "Scarlet?"

"You don't think it's a little insulting to ask me out the day before? You don't think I would have other plans already?"

"We only started this class today," he countered. "If we'd started on Monday, I would've asked you then." Although he'd would've asked her for Tuesday, but he wasn't about to tell her that. "Do you have plans for Saturday night?"

"Yes, I do."

He wasn't sure what to say. Should he ask her for the following Saturday?

"Start over," she said, then hung up.

He decided to make her wait. When he finally redialed fifteen minutes later, he got her voice mail.

"Ms. Elliott," he said, starting from the beginning. "This is John Harlan. We met at the *Charisma* open house over the holidays. I was wondering if you'd like to have dinner with me a week from Saturday. Here's my private line." He recited his phone number. "I look forward to hearing from you."

He'd barely hung up when his private line rang.

"It's a good thing I came into your life," Scarlet said. "Has that method worked in the past?" She said *method* as if it were something that stank.

"What method?"

"Leave a message for a woman asking her on a first date?"

She sounded either shocked or disgusted.

"I asked for more than a week from now."

"You asked her answering machine."

He massaged the bridge of his nose and closed his eyes. "Which is apparently the wrong thing to do. I'll start over," he said, hanging up before she could. Normally he would've been frustrated by that kind of game by now, but he found it stimulating. She challenged him. The trick would be to challenge her in return.

He lifted the receiver, then hesitated. She would be expecting him to call back.

"Not this time, Ms. Elliott," he said as he flipped through his Rolodex. He wanted an A on his first homework assignment.

She'd gotten him thinking outside his normal box. He wanted her to see what he'd already learned.

* * *

"Somebody likes you," a woman said as she rounded Scarlet's cubicle.

She smelled the flowers before she even looked up from her computer and spotted the bouquet, not something neat and tidy like a dozen roses, but an exotic bundle of baby orchids in a variety of deep colors. Her heart did a little dance at the sight. She hadn't been sent flowers in a long, long time. Even so, she resisted the temptation to bury her face in the blossoms as the vase was set down in front of her by Jessie Clayton, the vivacious twenty-three-year-old intern assigned to work with her.

"Shall I read the card?" Jessie asked, green eyes sparkling behind trendy glasses as she snagged the tiny envelope and held it over Scarlet's head.

"I write your performance reviews."

Jessie laughed and handed Scarlet the card. "I don't suppose you're going to read it out loud."

"Good guess."

Alone, Scarlet held the envelope to her lips for several seconds before opening it. Inside was a phone number. No flowery sentiment. No invitation to dinner. Just a phone number.

She smiled, slowly. Score one for John.

She picked up the phone and dialed.

"John Harlan."

She heard expectation in his voice, maybe because he was trying to cover it. "Nice move."

"Who's calling?"

She grinned. "Let me start over." She hung up and redialed. After he answered, she said, "The flowers are exquisite. Thank you."

"So you remember me?"

She slipped into the role. "Of course. We met at the *Charisma* open house over the holidays."

"You were wearing a green dress the color of your eyes," he said.

Her breath caught, even though they were talking about an imaginary occasion. He made it sound real, as if he'd seen and admired her in that dress. "You were wearing a suit and tie," she countered.

"Lucky guess. I hope you're wondering why I sent the flowers."

"I'm curious, yes."

"I'd like to get to know you. Would you have dinner with me? Maybe a week from Saturday?"

"I'd love to."

"May I pick you up, say, at eight o'clock?"

"That would be perfect."

"I'll call you during the week to reconfirm."

"Okay."

He said goodbye and hung up, and she was left wondering if he meant they wouldn't talk to each other or see each other until he picked her up. Was that how far the role-playing would go? Or would they have a separate life, continuing what they'd started?

For now she would let him lead the relationship. She would go to The Tides for the weekend to visit Gram and Granddad, as planned; attend the Spring Fling at the country club; and make herself unavailable to John, letting absence do its work.

Which was crazy, since nothing long-term could come of this relationship, anyway. But for the month that Summer would be out of town, Scarlet would indulge herself with the man who should be most forbidden to her and make herself a memory.

Five

Since the tragic day when Scarlet and Summer were orphaned, Scarlet had never spent an entire weekend at The Tides without her sister. It was strange now to be in her own bedroom and know that Summer wasn't just a few feet away in hers, or sharing a room as they got ready for a special occasion. The tomblike quiet was eerie.

Scarlet took a final look in the mirror and gave herself the okay sign, something Summer would've done. Once upon a time, Gram would have come in to share in the fun, too, but her arthritis prevented her from climbing the stairs easily anymore. She and Granddad had moved downstairs. Why they hadn't installed an elevator was a mystery to Scarlet.

Her heels tapped softly as she descended the long marble staircase to the first floor. She looked forward to the evening, even though she was dateless. She would know many of the guests, however, and would surely be asked to dance.

She was glad she hadn't told John where she was going. He might have decided to show up, and she wasn't sure she could pretend not to notice him.

Scarlet headed toward the back of the house to the living room, beyond which was her grandparents' suite. As Scarlet neared, her grandmother came out her bedroom door, carrying herself with the grace of a queen, a far cry from the seamstress she'd been when Patrick had first met her in Ireland and swept her off her feet, bringing her to his home in America. Her face barely showed age or tragedy, even at seventy-five and having suffered the loss of several children through miscarriage or death.

"Aren't you enchanting, *colleen,*" she said as Scarlet hugged her. "And dressed to stop lungs from pulling in air, I'm thinking. Your own creation?"

"Brand-new." Scarlet did a quick pirouette, showing off the snug violet-and-fuchsia sheath with the flounce that would swirl just above her knees when she danced. Three-inch heels brought her to six feet in height. She loved the additional height, which gave her a sense of power. "You're looking beautiful yourself, Gram."

Maeve wore a simple lavender beaded gown on her petite frame. Her makeup was applied deftly, a few freckles visible on her gorgeous Irish skin. She'd worn her white-and-auburn hair in an elegant updo for as long as Scarlet could remember, and it was no different now. As usual, too, a gold locket hung around her neck, rumored to hold a picture of her daughter Anna, her secondborn, who had died of cancer when she was seven. Scarlet wondered if the locket also contained a picture of her thirdborn, Stephen, Scarlet and Summer's father.

"Looking to turn a few heads, are you?" Patrick Elliott boomed from behind them.

In her heels Scarlet met her grandfather eye to eye, yet another reason she liked wearing them.

At seventy-seven Patrick was still a sight to behold. His fit body, thick gray hair and blue eyes continued to draw glances from women thirty years younger. "I'm hoping to, yes," Scarlet said.

"I was talking to your grandmother, missy." He tempered the comment with a slight smile at Scarlet, which turned tender when he looked at his wife and kissed her cheek. "You look lovely, *cushla macree.*"

Pulse of my heart. Scarlet had heard him call her grandmother that forever, had always found it hard to believe that this adoring husband was the same dictator who'd raised her and Summer. And as a businessman, he was ruthless—even, or more accurately *especially,* with his children, who ran four of his various enterprises.

"Are you taking your own car?" Patrick asked Scarlet. "I'm sure you'll want to stay longer than your grandmother and I."

"I'll ride with you. If I'm not ready to come home when you are, I'll get someone to drop me off."

"We'll send Frederick back for you," Gram said.

"Thanks, but it won't be necessary." Scarlet recognized she was being stubborn out of habit. Her grandparents' driver would be happy to make a second trip to pick her up. Still, she found it hard to alter the long-

established adversarial relationship with her grandfather. "I'll make my own way."

"Make sure your escort hasn't been drinking." He put
his hand under Maeve's arm as they moved toward the
door.

Scarlet brought up the rear, irritated that her grandfather assumed a man would bring her home. "I'll make
him take a Breathalyzer."

Maeve chuckled, which stopped Patrick from coun-
tering with something equally sarcastic. "So alike, you
two," Maeve said.

"Alike? Us?" Scarlet wasn't as stunned as she pre-
tended.

"Yes, *colleen*. But enough of this. It's a night to cel-
ebrate the arrival of spring. New beginnings. Let's have
no more battles of wit, no matter how clever the words."

"Fine by me," Scarlet said.

Patrick said nothing, which was answer enough. He
would do whatever Maeve asked of him.

Scarlet stopped short of heaving a sigh. She and
Granddad had butted heads forever, with Gram and
Summer interceding when possible. Her grandfather
had never liked any of her boyfriends, even during her
first tender explorations into the dating world, and so
she had begun to bring home guys she was sure he
would despise—men without much motivation or am-
bition, men whose main interest in life was having fun,
not working. Nothing turned off Patrick Elliott more
than a man without a solid work ethic, especially since
he had built his own empire from nothing.

Scarlet was tired of the game, though, and tired of
being at odds with her grandfather, especially now. He

must be feeling less invincible these days or else he wouldn't have given his children the challenge that the next CEO of Elliott Publication Holdings would be the person who produced for their magazine the biggest individual financial success by year's end. His surprise announcement at a New Year's party that he would be retiring, and the game he'd begun by pitting the Elliott children against each other, had turned all their lives upside down—a typical Patrick Elliott move.

During the twenty-minute limo ride to the country club, the conversation turned to safe topics, setting a new, peaceful tone for the evening. The club ballroom was decorated for the Spring Fling as it always was, with spring-flower arrangements and tiny white lights everywhere, nothing overly original or creative. A sumptuous buffet would be laid out, bars set up in convenient places, with dancing to come later, a twenty-piece band providing music. Scarlet loved its predictability.

"You look like an exotic bloom," Gram said as they waved and nodded to friends and acquaintances. "Your talent for design is staggering."

"I learned from the best." Scarlet put an arm around her grandmother, remembering fondly the hours and hours they'd spent sewing.

"That's a fine compliment, indeed, but I never had the vision, just the practical skill. I always expected you'd go into that field instead of the magazine, especially with your degree in design." Her sideways glance probed.

"I've got time. And the magazine's a useful place to learn more," Scarlet said evasively, wondering if Granddad had overheard. He didn't indicate outwardly that he had; in fact, he seemed focused on something across the room. She followed his gaze, spying the couple she'd most wanted to avoid.

She leaned closer to her grandmother. "Bill and Greta Harlan are here. Have you seen them since Summer called off the engagement?"

"I called Greta. As you know, we weren't great friends before John and Summer decided to marry. If you're wondering whether everyone will be civil, the answer is yes. Especially here. Now then, be off and enjoy yourself."

"I'll join you for supper later."

"You're not to feel obligated. Have fun, *colleen*. I don't think you're having enough fun these days."

"I miss Summer."

"And you're a mite envious, perhaps?"

"Not at all." Scarlet waited for lightning to strike her at the lie, but the world stayed normal. She did envy that Summer could be public with her relationship—and with a man she could count on and keep, whereas Scarlet was setting herself up for heartbreak, one she could never talk about or get sympathy for when it ended. But she wasn't jealous of her sister's happiness.

Scarlet wandered around the festive room, stopping to talk, admiring baby pictures thrust in her face from old friends settling down. She'd attended a record number of weddings in the past few years.

Gram was right. She wasn't having enough fun. Maybe it was because Summer wasn't there, and she was Scarlet's best friend. Maybe because Scarlet lived in Manhattan most of the time, and the country club now seemed too laid-back and…rigid, even though that seemed contradictory. Rules, rules, rules. She'd grown up with them, ignored them, gotten into trouble when she did. There were fewer rules in the city, more action, more options.

After dinner the dancing began. She watched her grandparents take the floor for the first slow dance, their steps perfectly matched after so many years of dancing together. Scarlet smiled as she watched them—until she spotted John walking onto the dance floor.

The lightning she'd expected before struck her, although for entirely different reasons. Everything inside her came feverishly to life. He was the best-looking man in the room. And she'd made love with him. And he'd wanted her, bad.

Okay, so she *was* glad he'd shown up. Admitting she had a problem was half the battle, she thought, being honest with herself. Then she saw a petite blonde step into his arms. Who was she? They waltzed together like long-time partners, their steps perfectly attuned, his hand resting at the small of her back, his gaze on her. He said something and the blonde laughed. Scarlet hated her.

The music went upbeat, and her grandparents left the dance floor, but John and his partner didn't. Scarlet tapped her toe. Was he trying to make her jealous?

"Hey, Scarlet."

She focused on the man who'd approached invisibly through her green haze. "Mitch, hi. Long time."

Mitchell Devereaux was as handsome as he was shallow, which was a lot.

"Yeah. Wanna dance?"

She certainly didn't want to sit on the sidelines,

watching. She would ignore John and have fun, as Gram had ordered.

Scarlet didn't leave the dance floor after that, changing partners with each new song, dancing her heart out and keeping a casual eye on John, who also didn't sit out a dance until the music slowed again, although he finally changed partners. Over her own dancing partner's shoulder she watched John stroll away, get a drink from the bar then prop a shoulder against a pillar and scan the dance floor, stopping on her, catching her looking at him.

He lifted his glass slightly, his gaze intense. She could hardly believe she knew what he looked like naked, what his skin felt like, tasted like. How he kissed as if he were being sent to war, and how he made love as if she were the only woman on earth.

The song ended. She made an excuse to leave the dance floor and headed toward him, pulled by a force stronger than her own willpower. Discreetly she pointed to a side door. He pushed away from the pillar and headed there. She followed at a distance, but as she passed through the door she saw her grandfather, apparently already on the patio, approach him.

Almost caught, Scarlet darted behind a pillar topped by a plant large enough to hide her.

"I never expected it from you, John," Patrick said.

"Expected what?"

"Retaliation."

"It's business, Patrick. Nothing more."

Scarlet wished she could see them, analyze their body language. All she could do was listen. Granddad's voice cut through the darkness, sharp and lethal. John seemed unaffected.

"Gills and Marsh have bought ad space in *Charisma* since the magazine debuted," Patrick said. "Crystal Crème soda has been with *The Buzz* for five years."

"A lot of my clients have decided to experiment with other forms of advertising, to see what gets them the most bang for their buck. Product placement in movies and on television guarantees a bigger, wider audience, not only in initial viewing but in DVDs and reruns."

"With the target demographics?"

"We're choosing each situation carefully."

The sound of crickets filled a long silence.

"You must be angry with my granddaughter," Patrick finally said.

"I'm over it."

"I don't think you are."

Scarlet leaned closer, as her grandfather's voice had gone low and cool.

"What makes you say that?" John asked.

"The way you were watching Scarlet a few minutes ago…. That wasn't the expression of someone who was 'over it.'"

"You're wrong. But even if I hadn't stopped caring about Summer, I wouldn't take it out on my clients—or Scarlet. Or you."

Another silence ensued. John didn't take the bait. Scarlet was grateful her grandfather hadn't realized John's expression was one of lust, not anger.

"Don't know what got into that girl," Patrick said at last. "She always had such a good head on her shoulders. Now she's run off with that…that singer. Left her job."

Exasperation coated the words. John still said nothing.

"I'm going to keep a close eye on all your accounts, John. Might have to do a little wooing of my own."

Scarlet smiled at the word and figured John had, too.

"They pay me for sound advice," John said.

"We'll see how sound it is."

"It's a new day in advertising, Patrick. Time for changes."

"Maybe." He took a couple of steps then stopped.

Scarlet had to duck a little.

"I should've called you and apologized," Patrick said. "Thought about it. Just didn't do it."

"No need to, but thanks. It was between Summer and me."

"So it was. Good night."

"Good night, sir."

Scarlet eased farther around the pillar so her grandfather wouldn't see her as he passed by.

"You can come out," John said after a few seconds. "He's inside."

She moseyed over. "That was close."

"I'm surprised you risked being seen with me in the first place, Scarlet."

"That wouldn't be a scandal, just a reason for people to talk a little. Are you enjoying yourself?"

"Not particularly."

"You could've asked me to dance, you know."

He straightened. "You had a partner for every dance. I shouldn't cut in, should I?"

"Maybe."

His gaze intensified. "Consider this tonight's Woo U lesson. Yes or no?"

"Each situation has to be judged individually."

"I judged. I chose not to."

"Okay." Because he was right and there was nothing more to say, she changed the subject, twining her fingers so that she wouldn't touch him, though she *really* wanted to. "*Was* it strictly business, John? What my grandfather asked you about?"

"Yes."

"You would've done the same thing, switched the business, if you and Summer were still engaged?"

He hesitated no longer than a breath, and his gaze never wavered. "Yes."

She wondered if he'd paused because he had to justify his answer to himself first.

"Wanna blow this joint?" he asked, surprising her.

"More than I can tell you. But impossible, as you know, at least together. I'd better go." She started to turn.

"Scarlet?"

His husky voice would've stopped her, no matter what he said next. "What?"

"I was jealous of every guy you danced with tonight, every guy who touched you and got to be so close to you."

Desire flooded her body…rushing…pounding…pulsating. His gaze drifted down her. Her nipples drew taut. She wasn't used to having a man want her so passionately, so…violently. It fascinated her, both that he wanted her that much and that she liked his Neanderthal reaction. She'd never tolerated jealousy before, but the flare of heat low in her body told her *his* jealousy meant something.

"You don't think I felt the same?" she asked. "I have to go." She wouldn't risk staying any longer with him, having someone see their attraction instead of just acquaintances having a conversation, or whatever defined the parameters of their relationship now in the public eye.

He said nothing. He was good at that.

She didn't see him return to the dance, and was torn between gratitude and disappointment as Mitch again invited her to dance. She saw her grandparents come onto the floor, as well, as Glenn Miller's "Moonlight Serenade" played, Gram's favorite.

A few seconds later, John tapped Mitch's shoulder. Mitch looked at Scarlet. "You don't have to."

"It's fine." Her heart thundered as John's arms came around her. Several inches of space separated their bodies.

"What are you doing?" she whispered, pasting on a smile.

"Passing another Woo U course."

"I can't believe you did that."

"Then you don't know me."

She didn't. She loved him, but she didn't know him. Not really. But everything she learned about him only deepened her feelings.

"Scarlet, there's no reason we can't be civilized in the world's eyes. So, there'll be a little talk. It'd mostly be about me and that I must still be pining for Summer."

"Are you?"

"No."

It was one of the most awkward moments of her life. She glanced at her grandparents. Gram lifted her brows. Granddad kept a carefully blank expression.

And yet through all the awkwardness, all the awareness of eyes focused on them, all the annoyance at being the center of attention when she'd tried so hard to stop doing that, she loved that he'd done it. Loved that he was that self-confident and daring. She never would've guessed it of him.

At the end of the dance the club manager approached Scarlet. "You have a phone call, Miss Elliott."

"From whom?"

"I wouldn't know. If you'll follow me, please."

She excused herself from John, grateful that the potentially awkward moment of moving off the dance floor and away from each other had been solved by a mysterious phone call.

She and the manager went down a long hallway to a door marked Conference Room. He opened the door then walked away. Scarlet peered in. A phone sat on the conference table but no light blinked. Uneasy, she took a step back.

"Careful," came a whisper in her ear. John. He moved her inside the room, shut the door and locked it, the sound echoing like a prelude to gothic seduction.

He slid a hand along the wall beside her, then the lights went out, plunging them into darkness. Music drifted faintly through the closed door.

"You dance like you make love," he said, dragging a finger along her jaw, across her mouth.

"How's that?" Breathless, she parted her lips.

"Primal. Like a creature of the earth. With passion and abandon." He slipped his arms around her waist. "Dance with me. A real dance."

"Dance" was a relative term. They barely moved. It was just an excuse to align their bodies, and since in her heels she was as tall as he, their bodies aligned perfectly.

"You're quiet," Scarlet murmured after a while.

"Some of us are capable of it."

She nipped his earlobe, and he laughed softly. She'd needed this moment alone with him. Needed to touch him. The music stopped, but they kept moving, pressed together, their clothing the only barrier, and even that wasn't much. He curved his hands over her rear and lifted her slightly, changing the point of contact. Perfume and aftershave mingled with the urgent scent of desire. His need was evident in the tautness of his body and the hard ridge pressed to her abdomen. His breath felt hot and unsteady against her temple.

Scarlet tried to resist. She couldn't abandon herself to him, all too aware of where they were and the possibility of discovery. She wouldn't do that to her grandparents or Summer. Or herself.

But she had a hard time not letting go, giving in, enjoying....

His hand slipped over her breast just as his mouth took hers in a long, hot kiss, a merging of breath and need and unchecked lust. They were always in such a hurry with each other.

He moved her back until her thighs hit the table. She realized what he intended and pushed at his chest.

"We can't do this here."

He trailed her low V neckline with his tongue, leaving a damp, shivery trail. "I'm familiar with the long list of rules this club has," he said. "Nowhere does it say there can't be sex in the conference room. In fact, I would hazard a guess that this room has seen plenty of action."

"Stop." She slipped away from him and found her way to the door, then fumbled for the light switch, turning it on. "I mean it. We can't do this here." She blamed herself for letting things get out of hand. The speed at which they'd landed in bed before this— twice—would have led any man to think he could have what he wanted, whenever he wanted it.

He shoved his hands through his hair. "You're hard to figure out," he said, then blew out a breath.

"I know. I'm sorry." *But I love you, and that's why I took those chances the other times. I needed a memory of you.*

"You don't really live up to your reputation, do you?" he said, half sitting on the table, his arms crossed.

"Do you want me to?"

After a few long seconds he shook his head.

She thought about her grandfather, how much she'd disappointed him. As a teenager she'd desperately wanted his attention, and he'd been totally focused on his business, but his disapproval of her dates meant he would at least communicate with her, if only to berate her. She was such a cliché, she thought.

"I always found the 'wild-child' tales interesting," John continued, "because there was no hard evidence you were easy, just speculation, based on who you dated—and maybe how you dress in look-at-me outfits and move like a whirlwind, as if you always know where you're going and who you are, which is very sexy. I'd say you pretty much made everyone wonder."

"I'm not the one who arranged this tryst."

"I didn't mean to offend you, Scarlet. I thought you would want it as much as I did."

"Believe it or not, sometimes I think about other people before my own needs."

His gaze locked with hers. He studied her for a long,

quiet moment, then he nodded slowly and stood. He ran a hand down her arm as he passed by.

"Good night," he said. "Thank you for the dance."

After the door closed quietly behind him she stood motionless, waiting for her world to return to normal.

She'd misread him, pure and simple. And maybe he'd misread her. It was her manufactured reputation that had driven him to take such a chance as to want to have sex with her on a conference room table with hundreds of people—her grandparents included—nearby.

Maybe he got a rush out of such clandestine moments.

She didn't. She'd only gotten a rush out of *him*.

So where did that leave them now?

Six

On the Wednesday after the country club incident, John arrived a few minutes early for a three o'clock meeting with Finola Elliott at *Charisma* magazine. He wasn't made to wait in the lobby but was escorted immediately to Fin's office by an auburn-haired young woman named Jessie, who kept up a running commentary as they wove through the maze of cubicles. He learned she'd been raised in Colorado, was an unpaid intern and a roommate of a *Charisma* proofreader, Lanie Sinclair. And by the way Jessie eyed him curiously, he guessed she knew he'd been engaged to Summer.

He wished he could ask her which cubicle was Scarlet's. If he could just look into her eyes, he'd know where things stood between them. They hadn't spoken since the disaster at the club. In three days they were supposed to go on their first Woo U date.

Or were they?

Maybe his lesson had been only in how to ask a woman out, not the actual follow-through. Another question he needed answered.

Who would break the stalemate? Or had they already burned out? He wasn't ready to end it. He wanted the whole month until Summer returned. Every last minute. And he wanted some of that in bed.

John wasn't taken into Fin's office but to the conference room attached to it. Several people were seated at the oval mahogany table—the editor in chief, Fin; her executive editor, Cade McMann; Bridget Elliott, the photo editor…and Scarlet.

He'd never been to a meeting with Scarlet in attendance before. Why would an assistant fashion editor be there?

John shook hands with Fin, Cade and Bridget. He met Scarlet's gaze directly and nodded. She raised her brows. No clue there as to how she felt.

"I'm not going to beat around the bush, John," Fin said. "I'm sure you've heard about the competition my father instituted."

"I'm aware of the details." Having just seen Maeve over the weekend, John realized how much Fin looked like her mother, although she had Patrick's head—and drive—for business.

"I intend to win." She leaned toward him, her body rigid. "But I can't if you keep pulling ad revenue from my profits."

"I'm responding to what my clients' needs are, Fin."

"We came up with an idea we'd like to toss out at you. Go ahead, Scarlet."

Scarlet picked up a remote control. She gave him a quick look, all business, which might have worked had she been wearing a gray, pin-striped, baggy suit and her hair in a bun. Maybe. As it was, her shiny hair curled softly over her shoulders, and she wore a deep purple dress that clung to every shapely inch of her. His mind wandered....

She brought up an image on the big-screen monitor on the wall. "Picture this as a feature article. We might call it 'Trends,' or something like that," Scarlet said. "Ten to twelve photos of the hottest trends for each season, as we generally do. But this is an example of how we would incorporate your clients' products."

A hip blond model was seated at a bar in what looked to be a neighborhood pub. She wore an outfit meant to draw the magazine reader's eye, but in her hand was a bottle of Crystal Crème soda. The juxtaposition of a soft drink being served at a bar would make the reader pay even more attention, he decided. Very clever.

"Product placement," Scarlet said unnecessarily. "Here are a few more."

Images flashed across the screen, each photo the superb quality that *Charisma* was known for, and each including a product of one of his clients, generally a food or drink item, easily integrated into the scene.

Cade pushed a folder toward John. "Price guides. You'll find it cheaper than a full-page ad, of course, but a fair price, we think, for the value."

Scarlet handed him a manila envelope. "Here's a CD of each sample so you can pitch your clients with visuals. These are mock-ups, obviously. We'd have to work closely together, matching our focus for the article with your product for the layout. Some products will lend themselves easily, but some won't. Some of these products have never been advertised in *Charisma*, like Crystal Crème. We think it opens a lot of new doors."

"You know that once you start down this path, you won't be able to go back," John said, skimming the price sheets. "And you'll be accused of selling out."

"We've talked it over," Cade answered. "Analyzed it. Had a few hearty debates, too. It's no different from a television program or movie showcasing products."

"It's not as if it's something new in the business," John said. "But it *is* new for you. Something you've resisted because of the ethics involved."

"It's a new day," Scarlet said. "A time for change."

She'd parroted what she'd overheard him say to Patrick the past weekend.

"We ask one thing, John," Fin said. "We want an exclusive. You don't go to the other EPH magazines—or anyone else—asking for the same thing. Let us run with it first."

John nodded. "Unless they ask. I can't pass up reasonable business, either, Fin. And I want an exclusive, as well. You don't offer this opportunity to anyone else for a few months, either."

"Fair enough," Fin said. "I've asked Scarlet to be your liaison on this project. Does that work for you?"

He didn't dare look at Scarlet. "Sure."

"She came up with a list of your clients whose products might be suitable for us."

"That's very competent of her."

A momentary silence hung over the room, then Fin

said coolly, "We're pleased we found a way to keep your business at *Charisma*."

"So am I." And now he and Scarlet would work together as well as play together, if that was what they could call it. But this business relationship would extend beyond the month.

"If you have time to stay and talk with her now, we would appreciate it."

"I do."

"Good." Finola rose, as did Cade and Bridget. "We'll be in touch."

The room emptied except for Scarlet and John, who sat across the wide table from each other.

"Your concept?" he asked her.

"Does it matter?"

"Just curious. I couldn't figure out why an assistant fashion editor was in on an ad meeting. If you came up with the idea, it makes sense that you would be here. Seems to me, though, that you'd like to take credit for something so daring for *Charisma*."

Scarlet sat back in her chair, her arms crossed. "Fin's a great boss. She's turned us into a team where credit *and* blame are shared."

"I've known her for a few years. This is the most on edge I've seen her."

"The competition." Scarlet shrugged. "Everyone's feeling the pressure."

"You think she should be the one to win? The one to become CEO of EPH, over your uncles?"

"I don't work for them." She smiled sweetly. "Here's the list." She skated it across the table.

He caught it, stood and walked around the table, not

taking his eyes off her. She watched him, as well. He sat beside her, close enough that her perfume drifted across the space between them. Her signature scent aroused him instantly.

"Are we still on for Saturday night?" he asked.

The door opened. Jessie shouldered her way in, carrying a tray with bottled water and glasses of ice. "Cade said I should sit in on your meeting."

"Great," Scarlet said with a little too much enthusiasm.

Saved by the intern. John could see the thought flash through Scarlet's mind.

And because he wasn't going to take no for an answer, he decided to be creative himself.

John had been right about one thing, Scarlet thought a half hour later as they left the conference room and headed to her cubicle. She *did* want credit for her idea to keep his business at *Charisma*. Not for the glory— she was a team player—but she wished her grandfather knew what she'd come up with. She wanted him to see that she was valuable to the magazine, not just an Elliott being given a position because of the family name.

As long as she was being honest with herself, she admitted she wanted John to know, too, because she needed him to acknowledge her abilities. It was unlike her to crave approval. What did that say about her? A sign of a new maturity...or insecurity? She wished Summer was home so they could talk about it, at least the part about Granddad. But their phone conversations, frequent but short, never allowed time for deep discussion, plus Summer was living a dream. Scarlet didn't want to wake her with reality yet.

Scarlet knew John was right behind her as they reached her cubicle, but his footsteps were almost silent. Sneaky. He was sneaky in a lot of ways. Good ways, interesting ways, like his card with the flowers that had only his phone number printed on it. Like luring her to the conference room at the Spring Fling. Like disguising his incredible body with boring suits. Outwardly he needed some flair to match what he was inside, which was fascinating.

The orchids he'd sent were still fresh, the vase overflowing with the wondrous blooms. She saw his gaze land on them.

She thumbed through a stack of papers on her desk, pulling out the one she wanted to give him.

"Thanks," he said. He stuffed the sheet into his briefcase. "I'll be in touch as I meet with each client."

He left. Just like that. Without finalizing plans for Saturday night, even though he'd asked her before.

An assortment of possibilities about how she could do him bodily harm ran through her head. Had he forgotten or was he playing a game with her? Maybe he was unhappy that they would be working together on the same project for an indefinite period of time.

Any other man might—

She stopped. Sat down. Set her elbows on her desk and rested her chin in her hands. John wasn't like any other man. And that was the problem.

She was used to leading a relationship, had thought *she* was letting *him* lead. But the fact of the matter was, he wasn't…leadable.

At five o'clock she headed to the elevator bank, grateful she wasn't an executive, whose work hours often stretched long into the night, even more so since Granddad had fired the starting gun on the competition. She was worried about Aunt Finny, who was way too tense, and determined to win, and was spending far too much time in the office these days.

"Scarlet!" Jessie ran up to her at the elevator, holding tight to a red helium-filled balloon. "This just came. There wasn't a card, but the delivery guy said it was for you."

Scarlet spied a piece of paper inside the balloon. She had no doubt who'd sent it.

But what did the note say?

"Thanks," she said to Jessie, leaving her curiosity unsatisfied as Scarlet stepped into the waiting elevator. "See you tomorrow."

She strode down Park Avenue, the string wrapped securely around her hand, the balloon hovering just above her head. She smiled as she walked. People smiled back. It was a drizzly spring day, but it was beautiful.

The man learned fast, she thought. He could've talked to her while they were in her cubicle, or called her after he'd returned to his office. Instead he sent her a balloon. How imaginative. Maybe it held a little apology for last Saturday night, as well as a reminder of the upcoming Saturday night.

She hailed a cab, lucky to find one unoccupied. Then at the town house she swung open the gate and headed for the door to the underground pool and garage to get to her private entrance. The sound of someone knocking on a window caught her attention. She spied her grandmother waving at her, motioning her to come through the front door.

Gram rarely came into the city anymore unless she was going on a shopping binge, in which case she made arrangements to shop with Scarlet in tow. They always made a day of it.

Curious why Gram hadn't alerted Scarlet that she was coming, Scarlet climbed the front stairs and walked into the entry, where a grand piano held center stage. When someone played, the sound reverberated through the entire three-story house.

"What are you doing here?" she asked her grandmother as they hugged.

"We have tickets for the opera. We came early so that Patrick could go into the office." She smiled at the balloon. "It's a special occasion, then, is it?"

"What? Oh, someone was passing them out. They're advertising something."

Maeve's brows lifted. "And you carried it all the way home?"

Scarlet shrugged, trying to look innocent. "It suited my mood."

"Why don't you pop it and see what's inside?"

"I, um, don't really care what's inside. I'd like to enjoy the balloon for a while."

Gram's eyes held a secret smile. "If you don't want to share the note, just say so, *colleen*. I respect your privacy."

Then for no fathomable reason the balloon popped on its own and the note went flying, landing faceup at Maeve's feet. Scarlet grabbed it before her grandmother could bend down, then held it up to read.

I look forward to Saturday night. Pick you up at eight.

Scarlet somehow managed not to sigh her relief at the

G-rated note, unsure whether her grandmother had had time to read it or not.

"So, you have a date tonight, then," Gram said, her eyes twinkling.

Scarlet looked at the note again. "No. Saturday."

Maeve pointed to it. "I think you've got a different message on the other side."

With dread Scarlet turned the note over. *Tonight. Nine. Be prepared for some lessons of your own.*

Gram laughed, softly at first, then with utter amusement at Scarlet's embarrassment.

"A healthy love life is a good thing. Is it anyone I know, then?"

Scarlet's face heated to broil. "Gram, please."

"Someone your granddad would approve of, for a change?"

She wished she could answer yes. Wished it with all her heart. But no one would be happy with her choice of John Harlan. No one.

Her grandmother patted her on the arm. "I won't tell Patrick, if that's your worry."

"I'm just not ready to talk about it."

"Sure, then, I'll leave it alone for now. Oh. We'll be taking the helicopter back to The Tides tonight, so you don't have to be worrying about us seeing your young man in the morning."

Like there was any way she would let John come over tonight, knowing that Patrick could change his mind and be there in the morning.

"Have a wonderful time at the opera," she said to her impish grandmother.

"I don't suppose you'll be visiting us this weekend?"

Scarlet laughed. "Good night." She headed to the indoor staircase, appreciating, as she always did, the calm, tasteful decor of the town house, decorated so similarly to The Tides. Maeve Elliott knew how to bring peace to a place—and a person.

When she reached her floor, she went straight into her room and dialed John's number.

"You got my balloon?" he asked, his voice full of sexy promise.

"My grandmother got your balloon."

"What?"

Good. At least she'd shocked him in return. "I was reading your lovely note about Saturday, while she was reading your more direct note on the other side."

The sharp, succinct curse that came next made her relax, although she didn't know why.

"What did she say?" he asked.

"That you could spend the night."

A long pause, then, "I beg your pardon?"

"You didn't sign your name to the note, so she doesn't know it's you specifically, but she made it clear that my young man could spend the night. She and Granddad are taking the copter home tonight."

A pause ensued. "I'm not willing to risk that," he said.

"Neither am I."

"Are you disappointed?"

She waited a couple of beats to answer him, not because she didn't know the answer but because she wasn't sure she wanted him to know exactly how disappointed she was.

"I'm going to take that as a yes. Saturday night is still a go, though, right?"

"Of course."

"Scarlet? About Saturday night… Is that to be a Woo U date, like a real first date?"

"You mean with no fringe benefits?"

"I'm just trying to know what to expect. Having two different—and opposite—relationships doesn't make things simple."

"It's a first date," she said. "We've already straightened out a few errors you've made in the past. Let's see if anything else needs fixing."

"All right."

She couldn't tell if he was disappointed, but she could guess. She didn't know how well she could stick to her own rules herself. She was still revved up from Saturday night at the country club. Just sitting next to him at the meeting today had made her wish they could find a dark corner somewhere and put an end to the aching need.

"Good night, John," she said as cheerfully as possible.

"'Night."

Scarlet changed into casual pants and a top, grabbed a leftover chicken Caesar salad from the refrigerator, then settled on the sofa with her sketch pad. She'd been unusually creative lately, ideas flowing so easily that she had already filled one pad and was halfway through another, in barely a month's time.

A psychologist would say she was sublimating—diverting her forbidden desire for John into a socially acceptable substitute, like designing an entire clothing line. After more than an hour she set aside her pad and wandered to the living-room window. People walked along the sidewalk, going to or coming home from dinner, probably. Singles moved along in haste. Couples strolled.

When was the last time she'd been on a date? Gone out to dinner with someone other than Summer or a girlfriend? Sometime during the past year she'd given up trying to irritate her grandfather by dating men he wouldn't approve of. She'd been asked out during that time, but had made excuses not to go.

Looking back, she realized she'd stopped dating when John and Summer had started getting serious, and Scarlet had begun falling in love with John. She'd spent a lot of time at home, sewing. Summer had been worried about her, had often invited her to come along with her and John. Scarlet had made so many excuses she'd run out of creative ideas.

The irony, of course, was that her grandfather would approve of John—if he hadn't once been engaged to Summer. Patrick wouldn't tolerate scandal. He'd even forced Aunt Finny at age fifteen to give up her baby born out of wedlock, in order to save public face. Scarlet figured Fin was fighting so hard to win Patrick's corporate game because she'd harbored so much resentment for him these twenty-plus years since having her baby taken away.

Scarlet didn't want to become like Fin. She wanted to make peace with Patrick. But there was no way she could make peace by pursuing John for anything beyond this month of stolen nights. People would talk too much, especially this soon after the breakup.

She wished she were brave enough to end the relationship now, but she wasn't. Only a couple more weeks, then the choice would be taken from her.

The phone rang, slicing into her thoughts, for which she was grateful.

"What do you think about using Une Nuit as a locale for a shoot?" John asked without saying hello. "Models seated at a table, looking at a menu, the name of the restaurant right there for the world to see."

"I think it could be considered a conflict of interest, since my cousin Bryan owns the place. Is he a client of yours now?"

"Brand-new."

"I thought Bryan liked to fly low under the radar. And last I heard he had reservations booked until the twelfth of never."

"I can't tell you what his plans are."

"Can't or don't know?"

"Take your pick."

She smiled. She liked a man who could keep confidences. "So, you're spending the evening working?"

"It was that or stand in a cold shower all night."

She burrowed into the sofa cushions, tucking the phone closer. "Were you serious in your note about having something to teach me?"

"That's for me to know and you to find out."

How in the world had Summer given up this man? Scarlet wondered for the thousandth time. He was quick-witted, funny, smart and sexy. What more could a woman want?

"Want to reschedule tonight's plan for Friday?" he asked.

"Can't. I have a meet and greet at Michael Thor's new studio," Scarlet said.

"It can't last all night."

"I promised Jessie I'd take her by Une Nuit afterward. I'm really sorry."

A beat passed. "So, that leaves us back at our Saturday night Woo U date," he said.

"Good thing you asked early," she said pertly, glad when he laughed. "John?"

"What?"

"I've been thinking." She waited for him to come back with some clever insult, but there was only silence. Maybe he heard the tension in her voice. "I'm not sure we should be doing more than just the Woo U stuff."

"Meaning?"

"We were lucky my grandparents didn't catch us tonight. Maybe that's a sign we shouldn't spend all that much time together."

"You believe in signs? Omens? Fate?" he asked.

"When it's convenient…or logical."

"Before we make such a big decision, why don't we sleep on it? We'll talk about it on Saturday. After the date ends."

Because she wanted to avoid the discussion herself, she said, "Works for me. Good night, John."

"Sweet dreams, Scarlet."

The way he said the words turned her to mush. She knew he had to be disappointed in her decision, yet he'd said his own good-night with tenderness in his voice, not impatience or irritation. Personally, she would've been irritated if he'd come to the same determination that she had.

She liked that she kept learning something new about him.

After a minute she glanced at the clock. She could change her mind right now—grab a cab and surprise him. He was at home and alone. He would satisfy her deprived needs….

Instead she took a warm bath and went to bed, in search of those elusive sweet dreams.

John printed the results of his evening at the computer, stacked the papers and put them in his briefcase. He started to pour himself a Glenfiddich, hesitated then went ahead and splashed some in a glass. The smooth, pricey scotch could've easily reminded him of the day Summer broke their engagement, but instead he chose to associate it with his first night with Scarlet.

He carried the glass with him to look out his window. It had started to rain sometime in the past hour. He turned off all the lights and stood, sipping and watching and remembering. The way she'd watched him undress. Her red bra and thong. The incredible sounds she made, flattering and arousing. Then the way she rushed away, leaving her coat behind. He'd sat on his bed, holding it to his nose, breathing in her scent for a long time after she was gone.

He hadn't expected to ever see her again, at least not like that. He'd been wrong.

And somehow he'd gotten himself into a position where they would spend hours together on Saturday without hope of ending up in bed. Maybe never sleep together again.

He really wondered whether he'd fried a whole lot of brain cells since he'd first slept with her. He knew he was infatuated, because she was rarely out of his mind. Even now he'd gone hard just thinking about her, a condition he hadn't experienced with this much uncontrolled regularity since he was a teenager.

It couldn't be more than lust. He refused to have his

heart broken by another Elliott woman. Or even have his life turned upside down.

But he wanted her....

To hell with it. He set his empty glass on the bar, grabbed his coat and keys and went out the door. He could sneak out of her house long before anyone was up to see him, convince her not to give up the sexual relationship.

But when the elevator doors opened he stared at the empty car until the doors closed. He returned to his apartment. His huge, quiet apartment. And went to bed alone.

Seven

Une Nuit buzzed no matter what night of the week, but this was Friday, and the crowd was different on Friday. Younger, even hipper, if that was possible. A visual sea of beautiful people dressed in New York's color of choice—black—enjoying the daring French/Asian fusion cuisine that was always being written up in the media, thus keeping the very trendy restaurant *the* place to be.

With Jessie in tow, Scarlet wove through the bar crowd at the front of the restaurant, looking for her cousin Bryan. While he might join them at dinner briefly, he generally wandered around the rest of the time, a hands-on owner.

She'd almost reached the maître d's podium when she came across Stash Martin, a wickedly handsome

Frenchman in his early thirties. As manager of Une Nuit, he was as much a fixture as Bryan.

"Scarlet, welcome," he said. They exchanged kisses on both cheeks.

"Crazy," she said, grinning, looking around.

"But quite typical. If you are looking for Bryan, he is not here. He is out of town. Again."

"Where does he go?" she asked rhetorically then introduced Stash to Jessie, who was wide-eyed at the scene. Bryan had always been an adventurer, even as he seemed to love his restaurant. He came and went a lot, but his business thrived because he had a staff he could count on.

"You would like a table, eh?" Stash asked.

"Any family members here?"

"Not a one. The Elliott table is free."

"What do you think?" Scarlet asked Jessie. "Table or the bar? How hungry are you?"

"Not very. The bar is fine."

"Wait here a moment," Stash said, then he approached the maître d'.

Scarlet had talked Jessie into borrowing an outfit from the closet of designer clothing at the magazine, but she hadn't been able to talk Jessie into letting her hair loose from the braid she always wore. The black leather pants and turtleneck did give her a different look, a fashionable one. Even Scarlet, usually a standout because of the colorful outfits she often wore, was wearing black—a miniskirt, boots and belted leather jacket. Her hair was pulled up into an untidy knot. She considered the look as just another aspect of her personality.

Stash returned then pointed to a couple sitting at the very center of the long, black lacquered bar. "Stand behind them. They'll be called in to dinner as soon as you make your way over there."

Scarlet flashed him a smile. "You're the best."

He lifted Scarlet's hand to kiss, and she fluttered her lashes playfully.

"When are you going to sleep with me and get me out of your system, *ma chérie?*" he asked, as he always did.

"Soon," she answered, as she always did.

A few minutes later she and Jessie were seated at the bar, waiting for their drinks.

"I've never seen anything like this," Jessie said in awe. "It's like a movie. Red and black and sexy. And I love the copper-topped tables."

"Maybe we'll order something to eat later, so that you can taste how incredible their food is." She smiled at the bartender when he placed an apple martini in front of her, then lifted her glass to Jessie. "To adventures in the big city."

"I wish I could afford more of them. Someday. When I have a paying job. Every penny of my savings is budgeted. Thanks so much for this treat."

"Keep performing well at *Charisma,* and you could be offered a paying job at the end of your internship." She sipped her drink then looked around, making eye contact with a man at the end of the bar, who toasted her. She smiled but looked away, then realized she shouldn't put up roadblocks, since Jessie might be interested. She decided to give him another chance, but Jessie's words stopped her.

"There's that man from the ad agency, John Harlan."

Surprise pelted Scarlet from all sides. "Where?"

"At a table behind you, in the corner."

She wasn't sure she wanted to turn around. If he was with a woman, she didn't want to know.

"He's looking right at you. I think he knows I'm telling you he's there," Jessie said in an emphatic whisper.

"Hmm." She took a long sip of her drink. He was courteous and would probably approach them at some point, especially since he and Jessie had taken note of each other. Scarlet would wait for him to initiate contact. Until then she could ignore the possibilities of whom he was with.

Maybe that blonde from the country club dance. She never had asked who that was.

"Is it true he was engaged to your sister?" Jessie asked.

Scarlet sighed. "They were engaged on Valentine's Day, but Summer called it off a couple of weeks later, just about the time you were hired."

"It must be weird for him, seeing you. Working with you, her identical twin."

Tell me about it. She'd wondered at the beginning if she was only a substitute for her sister, a way to get Summer out of his mind, but she didn't think that was true now. They had their own relationship. And while it was fun at times, she was always aware of the impending and necessary conclusion. They couldn't even just date and see where things might go. Even if Summer—and their grandfather—could somehow accept it, because of Scarlet's reputation, many people might assume that Scarlet had interfered somehow, even before Zeke Woodlow had appeared on the scene. It wasn't worth the grief.

Or was it?

The man from the end of the bar approached, saving Scarlet from coming up with an answer. Late twenties,

Scarlet decided. A little taller than she, blond and blue-eyed. He didn't look overly sophisticated or jaded, which meant he might work as a flirtation for the still-naive Jessie. Diverting her attention from watching John was a good idea.

"I'll bet you're sisters," the man said.

Scarlet met Jessie's gaze. She looked startled, but Scarlet smiled. "Coworkers," she said.

"I'm Rich."

"Money doesn't matter to me," Jessie said sincerely.

Scarlet grinned. "I think he means his name is Rich. That's Jessie. I'm Scarlet."

"I know who you are," Rich said to Scarlet, his hand resting on the back of her bar stool, almost touching her. "I saw your picture in the newspaper with Zeke Woodlow."

Scarlet angled closer to the bar. "That was an impersonator," she said, trying to make light of it. It had actually been Summer, dressed in Scarlet's clothes, made to look like a groupie. Scarlet held up her empty glass to the bartender.

"I'll get that," Rich said to the man.

"No, thank you." She decided she didn't want this guy around, after all. She caught Stash's eye, then tipped her head slightly toward Rich. Stash headed her way.

"Mon petit choux," he said, nudging Rich out of the way to kiss her, a little longer than was necessary for the ruse, Scarlet thought, wondering what John was thinking of the scene. "I apologize for keeping you waiting, *ma chérie,*" Stash continued, nuzzling her neck.

"Don't do it again." She leaned into him as he slipped an arm around her shoulders.

Rich was resourceful, however, and undeterred. He turned his attention on Jessie. "May I buy you a drink, um, Jenny?"

Jessie used her little straw to swirl her ice, then she slipped the straw in her mouth and pulled it out slowly, getting his attention. "You know, Rich, I believe my daddy would get a kick out of you."

He looked ready to swagger. "He would?"

"In fact, he has a saying that would fit you to a T. He'd say, 'That poor Rich. He's got nothin' under his hat but hair.'"

Scarlet had to set her drink down before the contents sloshed over the sides. Jessie's handling of Rich showed she wasn't quite as naive as she sometimes seemed.

"Bitch," he said, low and furious. "You—"

Stash moved but was blocked by John, who snatched the glass out of Rich's hand and thumped it on the bar next to Scarlet's. "Time to find a new watering hole, partner," John said, clamping a hand on his shoulder.

Rich glowered, but he left without comment, just a surly look.

"Are you okay?" John asked Jessie.

"I'm fine. Actually, it was kinda fun." She grinned.

Scarlet waited for him to turn his attention on her, but he said good-night and left. She watched him walk out the door, cross in front of the window and disappear. Only then did she look toward the corner where he'd been seated. Three women sat there.

"He had been alone," Stash whispered in her ear.

Scarlet tried to calm her nerves. She didn't know what to think about John. Was he mad? Jealous of Stash? Hurt?

She decided to change her outward mood since even Stash had picked up on something he shouldn't. "Thanks for the rescue. But, *mon petit choux?*"

"My little cabbage." His eyes twinkled. Jessie laughed.

"I know what it means."

"It is an endearment." He lifted a loose strand of hair over her ear. "Perhaps you ladies have had enough excitement and would like to have dinner now. I have kept the table for you."

Scarlet decided if she didn't take some time to think about John and how to handle what had just happened, she would probably do the wrong thing—like go after him. "I've worked up an appetite. How about you?" she asked Jessie.

"I could use a big ol' rib eye myself. There's nothing like dispatching a preening bull to give me an appetite."

Scarlet smiled. She was glad they'd gone out together. Glad she'd gotten to know Jessie better. "Would your father really have said something like that?"

"Oh, yeah. He's full of 'em."

"What does he do?" Stash asked as they reached their table.

"He's a cattle rancher."

"Do you rope and ride?"

"About as easily as breathing," she said.

His brows raised. "I have never before met a cowgirl." He asked a passing server to bring two menus.

"I'm going to use the restroom first," Jessie said to Scarlet then headed toward the back of the restaurant.

Scarlet hoped Stash wasn't going to comment on John's behavior, but she should've realized she wouldn't be that lucky.

"So. Your sister's fiancé."

"Ex-fiancé."

"And you."

"No. Just in the same place at the same time."

"T'es menteuse, toi."

"I'm not a liar." Technically, they weren't together. They were just enjoying each other's company briefly.

"He did not take his eyes off you from the moment he saw you."

She wished she had a menu to hide behind. "I have no control over John's actions."

He only smiled. "Bryan would want me to tell you your meal is on the house."

"He's my favorite cousin," Scarlet said sweetly.

Stash grinned and walked away.

Much later Scarlet and Jessie shared a cab home. Scarlet lived only a few blocks from Une Nuit and was dropped off first. Jessie continued on after thanking Scarlet profusely for the amazing night.

Scarlet headed up her stairs, questions running through her head. Should she call John? *Was* he angry? Was it better just to leave it alone for now?

She turned the landing of the third floor and spotted John leaning against the wall by her door. She slowed, studying his face, trying to guess his mood. She wanted to see him flash those dimples, but she didn't think there was much chance of that. He looked…single-minded.

He didn't move an inch when she approached. Her shoulder brushed his chest as she put her key in the lock. "What would you have done if I'd brought some-one up with me?" she asked mildly, her heart pounding.

"Discouraged him from going inside."

Scarlet opened the door and went in, leaving the door open but not inviting him. He came inside and shut the door.

She tossed her purse on an entry table then crossed her arms. "What do you want, John?"

"You know the answer to that."

"Short of *that,* what else?" The game, the words, excited her. She sensed he knew it, too.

"You ignored me."

"You ignored me, too," she said. It had confused her, angered her, that he'd spoken to Jessie at the bar but not her.

"You were cozy with Stash. I didn't want to interfere."

"Stash and I flirt with each other. It's nothing."

"I'm not telling you what to do or not to do. We don't have an exclusive relationship."

That hurt. Even if it lasted only the month, she'd thought it was exclusive.

"Well, fine, then. Because I don't explain myself to anyone." She turned away, not having a clue what to do next, just that she couldn't look at him.

"Look," he said, coming closer, touching her shoulder. She pulled away.

"This is not going the way I envisioned," he said, frustration in his voice. "I just wanted to clear the air before tomorrow night. I don't think I could have even a pretend date with you with tonight hanging over us."

"What is 'tonight' to you? Why are you angry?"

"You think it was easy watching you flirt with that jerk at the bar, then again with Stash? And you knew I was there. I know Jessie told you. Were you trying to make me jealous?"

She spun around. "The jerk came up on his own," she said, breaking her own rule about not explaining herself. "I sort of encouraged him because I thought he might work for Jessie. Then he showed his true, sleazy colors and I beckoned Stash to come over. I flirted with Stash so that there wouldn't be a scene, but the jerk was also stupid and things got out of hand, anyway. Stash is a friend. That's *all*."

"You could've beckoned *me*," John said quietly.

He was hurt? That was what his problem was? She closed her eyes for a moment. Since he was being honest with her, she could do the same. "I hadn't turned around at the bar. I didn't know if you were on a date. I didn't want to know."

"I would've come to your rescue regardless."

"Your date would've been unhappy about that."

He set his hands on her shoulders. "Why would I have taken a date to Une Nuit? You told me you were going to be there. Why would I do that to you?" He didn't wait for answer. "What kind of man do you usually go out with that you would think me capable of such rudeness?"

"Obviously a different kind of man. I'm working on changing that, however."

She saw him relax.

"I don't intentionally hurt people, Scarlet. I *am* civilized."

Maybe on the surface he was. He'd been raised well, raised to be civilized. But at moments like tonight and during their private tryst in the country club conference room, he wasn't completely civilized. She liked that about him. She loved that about him. She'd fallen in love months ago with the kind man who'd been so good to Summer, but now she'd fallen deeply, hopelessly in love with this fascinating man who was more primal than she'd expected, more intriguing, more complex. She liked that he'd been waiting for her when she got home, wanting to clear the air, even if the answers to his questions weren't what he wanted to hear. She liked that he faced things head-on.

She laid her hands on his chest and looked him in the eyes. Words didn't come, however. After the longest thirty seconds of her life, he lifted his hands and pulled out her hair clip, letting her hair fall around her face, then combed it with his fingers. He cupped her head, moved toward her. She suddenly wished she'd kicked off her shoes so that she could rise up on tiptoe to meet him. The idea made her smile.

"What?" he asked.

"You make me feel so...female."

One side of his mouth lifted. "Is that a good thing?"

"No one has made me feel like that before."

"Again, is that a good thing?"

"Yes."

"How have you felt before?"

"I don't know. Equal. Or sometimes even dominant." She didn't want to tell him more, didn't want to give him ammunition for teasing her. She just knew she felt different with him.

"You've been plenty dominant with me." He was still holding her head, keeping her close. His breath dusted her face. His beautiful dark brown eyes were filled with tenderness and need.

She smiled wider. "Not in comparison."

"Ah." He brushed his lips over hers once, twice, once more. "You make me feel different, too."

His mouth finally settled on hers, his tongue seeking hers. She wound her arms around him.

So much for resisting each other.

With a sigh she gave in to her needs, not attempting to stop the urgent sounds that rose from within her, which seemed to arouse him more. He pulled her close, slid a hand over her rear, tugging her against him, letting her feel his need. She moved her hips against him, and his kisses turned almost violent. He fisted her hair and tipped her head back, ran his tongue down her neck, his fingers frantically opening the belts and buckles on her jacket then shoving the jacket off her, hearing it land with a quiet thud. She was starved for him, had never wanted like this before, as if she could die if she didn't have him inside her immediately.

He fumbled with her zipper, then her skirt joined her jacket, leaving her in a sheer black bra, thong and boots. Her nipples were so hard, they hurt.

He took a step back to unbutton his shirt, dragged the tails free.

"When I'm ninety I will remember this," he said, low and harsh.

She hooked her hand in his waistband and brought him closer, wanting him, needing him. She knelt before him, pressed her mouth to his fly, his hard need flattering and exciting. She reached for his belt buckle—

The phone rang.

"The answering machine will get it," she murmured, placing both hands on him, watching his head fall back as she traced the length and breadth of him through the fabric.

Second ring.

He dragged her up, flicked open her bra and sent it flying.

Third ring.

He cupped her breasts, thumbed her nipples, sucked one into his mouth.

Fourth ring.

"We're not home. Leave a message," came Scarlet's own voice from the nearby machine.

"Hi, it's me!"

Summer.

John became like a statue.

"You must be out having fun. Maybe I'll call your cell after this. Haven't talked to you for a couple of days, and I'm missing you. Although not too much," she added with a laugh. "Scar, I can't tell you how happy I am. How incredible Zeke is. You've got to fall madly, passionately in love. You do. It's…it's indescribable."

John straightened, stepped away. He shoved his shirt into his pants. His eyes met Scarlet's. She felt naked, clear to her soul. She couldn't read his thoughts. He guarded his expression.

"Zeke, stop. I'm talking to my sister."

In the background came the rumble of a deep voice, but the words weren't clear.

John scooped up Scarlet's jacket. She turned around, letting him help her put it on. She tugged the edges together before she faced him again.

"I guess I won't call you on your cell, after all. I have something else—" Summer laughed "—to do at the moment. I'll catch you later. Bye. I miss you."

Scarlet didn't know what to say. She couldn't joke

about it—it wasn't the least bit funny. And making light of it wouldn't sit well with either of them.

As a reminder of the predetermined parameters of their risky relationship, it had a powerful effect. Resistance was the key. This time they needed to try harder.

Maybe her disappointment and fears were in her eyes, though, because John laid a hand tenderly along her face. She covered it with her own.

"Tomorrow night?" he asked.

She nodded. She wasn't going to miss any opportunity to see him, be with him.

He left with no kiss, no hug. Just a long, thorough, final look at her in her jacket, thong and boots.

For the first time in her life, she wished she didn't have a sister.

Eight

Saturday refused to pass by with any kind of speed. Scarlet picked out what she would wear on her Woo U date, pressed it, chose jewelry, then looked at the clock. Noon. She had hours and hours to fill. Normally she would spend her free time sewing, but not now. She was too keyed up, plus today was glorious, clear and crisp. She decided to walk the three miles to the EPH building and work out in the company gym.

At the gym Scarlet pushed herself until every muscle burned, then she showered, wrapped up in a towel and settled in the sauna. She wished she could say that she'd been able to block John from her thoughts, but she kept seeing the look on his face—or the nonlook—as Summer talked to the answering machine, and how quickly he'd left.

Not that she would've wanted to make love after that, either, but—

No *but*. There was nothing either of them could've done differently. Fate had intervened. For a moment—just a moment—she'd even thought they might have a chance for a future together.

The sauna door opened, and Fin came in. She was entitled to use the private executive section but hadn't chosen to. The four siblings being put through the wringer for the CEO job were straining to keep their familial ties, but it was more of a competition now than a family unit.

"Good workout?" Fin asked as she sat a few feet from Scarlet.

"I pushed myself hard. I needed it. Hadn't been here for a couple of weeks. I'm sure I'll pay for it tomorrow, though."

"I just had a massage from Magda. See if you can catch her before she leaves."

Scarlet stuck her head out the door, caught an employee passing by and made her request then sat again.

"I'm glad to see you taking care of yourself," Scarlet said to her aunt. "I worry about you. Everyone's worried about you."

"It's only a year out of my life. I'll manage. After I win, I'll take some time off." She leaned her head back and closed her eyes.

"Did you go home last night or sleep on the couch in your office?"

"Office," she said lazily. "Everything going okay with the new project?"

"Everything's great."

"It's comfortable working with John?"

"It's fine." Scarlet didn't want to get into it with Fin. "It's business."

"And how's the new intern working out?"

"Good. Jessie's got the eye, Fin. I think you should seriously consider keeping her on. She'll land someplace. Might as well be with us rather than with a competitor."

The door opened. "Ms. Elliott, Magda says if you can come now, she can give you forty-five minutes."

"Tell her I'll be right there, please."

She scooted close to her aunt and tapped her arm, making her open her eyes. "We all want you to win, Aunt Finny. But we all want you healthy when you do."

"I'll be fine. Go."

Scarlet made sure an attendant knew not to let Fin stay in there for more than fifteen minutes. She would undoubtedly sleep, and could easily end up in the sauna for hours without anyone knowing.

An hour later, exercised, steamed and massaged, Scarlet headed for the elevator, feeling utterly relaxed. She would go shoe shopping, she decided. It would help her pass the time.

"Ms. Elliott," said a gym attendant, running to catch up and sounding frantic as Scarlet waited for the elevator. "Your grandfather would like to see you."

To her credit, Scarlet didn't groan, but thanked the young man and hit the up button. If she hadn't taken time to indulge herself with a massage she would've been long gone by now. She sighed at her bad timing.

Scarlet had been to the twenty-third floor surprisingly few times in her life, and not at all since she'd been working at *Charisma*. Her grandfather's office was furnished in an old European style, like The Tides and the

Manhattan town house, with antiques that he and Gram had collected on their travels. The familiarity should've helped to make her feel comfortable, but it never had, not when the man himself was present.

Had Gram told him about the note in the balloon? She'd said she wouldn't, but...

Mrs. Bitton, his assistant/watchdog, wasn't at her desk, and the door to his inner office was open. She peeked in.

He was on the phone and waved her in.

"I will be there in time," he said gently into the telephone. "And I'm not working too hard, *cushla macree*. In fact, Scarlet just stopped by, so I'm going to visit with her for a while, then I'll head home."

Scarlet shook her head at his ability to twist things for his own purposes. As if she would just stop by on her own. Ha!

She wandered to the opposite wall to study a painting of her grandmother as a young bride. Most of the Elliott women took after her in one way or another. In this pose, Scarlet could see Fin's heritage directly.

"Prettiest woman on earth," her grandfather said, coming up beside her.

"Inside and out," Scarlet said.

"Why she's put up with me all these years only God knows."

Her instinct was to agree with him. Because of that, she didn't.

"No comment, missy?"

She smiled and shrugged. He invited her to sit in one of the wingback chairs in front of his desk. Surprisingly, he sat in the other instead of taking his position of authority behind the desk.

Hmm. He must not want to intimidate her this time. What was going on?

"Would you like something to drink?" he asked.

Curiouser and curiouser. "I'm fine, thanks. What's up, Granddad?"

"Are you dating anyone in particular these days?"

She went on full alert. "Why?"

"Just making conversation."

"Since when?" The words slipped out before she could stop them. She regretted being sarcastic, but his question worried her. Did he know about John? No. He would've been direct if he knew.

His lips compressed. "Can't I be interested in your life?"

"So, you're just making conversation? You really don't care if or who I'm dating, right?"

"Of course I do." He shifted in his chair, obviously uncomfortable.

"What if I told you I was dating, oh, say, John Harlan?" Was she stupid or brave to test him? she wondered.

"I would know you were just being obstinate about answering."

"Why?"

"You would never betray your sister like that."

Betray. Of all the reasons she'd come up with for why she couldn't see John beyond this month, it had never entered her mind that she would be betraying Summer. Summer had given up John. Period. Scarlet hadn't stolen him. But Granddad would see it as a betrayal, probably because it would be like shoving Summer's nose in her mistake, a reminder of how much she'd hurt another human being.

"Nor would John go out with you," he added. "Don't even joke about such a thing. Although I was surprised to see you dance with him."

Scarlet couldn't find words to reply.

"Okay, I can take a hint," he said after a few seconds. "No personal questions. I called you up here because I've been hearing good things about the job you're doing. Competent and creative, that's what people are saying. I wanted you to know I'm proud of you."

Scarlet was stunned into further silence. She couldn't remember her grandfather ever doling out compliments to her. "Thank you," she managed to say, fighting back the sting of tears.

"I'm looking to you now, Scarlet. Summer has gone off to live in sin with that rock star. Even if she does come back to work, she'll probably have babies soon. I think you'll stick around. You're not one to romanticize."

He shocked her anew, this time in a way that ticked her off. Did he think he was complimenting her by saying such a thing? "Meaning?" she asked.

"I think you're part of the future of EPH. Like your aunt, you'll devote yourself to your work."

Considering that Fin was driving herself to an early grave, Scarlet didn't consider her aunt's devotion something to strive for.

Then there was the other issue, how Scarlet wanted to be a designer, not an editor. How long would she have to pay family dues before she could do what she wanted? How much did she owe her grandfather for raising her after her parents had died?

"You're not usually so reluctant to argue with me, missy."

"Maybe I'm growing up."

"That's a welcome possibility."

She kept her expression serious. "It couldn't be because you're getting feeble, and I'm being careful not to cause you to have a heart attack or something."

His fists landed on his thighs. "Feeble?" he roared.

She drew a deep breath, exhaled slowly. Now this was the Granddad she knew and understood. She decided to take advantage of his bluster to kiss his cheek and leave while she had the upper hand. "Let's do this again sometime, Gramps."

She heard him chuckle as she walked through the door. It made her smile—until she got into the elevator and remembered his comment about betraying Summer. Summer wouldn't see it as a betrayal, but she would surely be uncomfortable. Adults made choices in life. Scarlet could choose to make things easy on her sister or difficult.

Without question, Scarlet would always make things easy for Summer—even to the point of denying herself love and passion, something Summer had found, and wanted Scarlet to find.

But probably not with John Harlan.

John knocked on Scarlet's door at precisely eight o'clock. He was nervous—seventeen-years-old, first-prom-date nervous. Which was stupid, since he'd already slept with her. How could he be tense about seeing her, making conversation now?

Because he had to act like he *hadn't* slept with her. Hadn't seen her incredible body in its natural state. Hadn't seen her face as an orgasm overtook her. Hadn't felt her hands and mouth all over him, hot and curious....

Okay. That line of thought had to be stopped right now, or else when she opened her front door she would see a bulge in his pants and he'd get his hand slapped with a ruler or something. The thought made him smile. Sister Scarlet. *There* was an image.

He saw the doorknob turn and tried to get himself into character. First date… First date.

"Hello, John," she said, looking soft and sweet in her buttoned-to-the-neck, electric-blue dress, her hair piled on top of her head but still looking touchable.

"Hi." He handed her a single white rose wrapped in green florist's paper and tied with a satin ribbon. He watched her bury her nose in it and smile. She looked nervous, too, he decided. It relaxed him.

"Thank you," she said. "It's lovely."

"Are you ready to go?" he asked.

"Let me put this in water and get my wrap. Come in."

He almost told her not to bother putting the rose in water, then decided not to spoil the surprise he had for her later.

She was Scarlet but not Scarlet, he thought, as she disappeared into her tiny kitchen. Her dress wasn't as daring as she generally wore, except that long line of buttons begged to be undone. Her jewelry was understated, and not as musical as usual. A couple of bangle bracelets that made a little noise, diamond studs instead of intertwining hoops in her ears, but that was all.

"I'm ready," she said, slipping a silvery wrap around her shoulders.

Should he tell her she looked beautiful? Was that kind of compliment encouraged at this point? Man, he felt like a kid.

"You changed your perfume," he said instead. It wasn't her usual citrusy scent, but tempting nonetheless. He couldn't put a name to the fragrance. Not flowery. Not powdery. He'd smelled them all in his years of dating. Scarlet's was just arousing.

She smiled. He guessed it was a good thing, noticing a detail like that.

He rested his fingertips lightly against her lower back as they left her apartment. It was going to drive him crazy not being able to touch her more than that all night. But he planned to kiss her good-night at her door later, a decent kiss, not a polite, end-of-evening peck. He didn't care if it messed up the Woo U curriculum at that point.

While in the car, they didn't speak beyond routine chitchat about the traffic and weather. The awkwardness of knowing what they did about each other, and pretending not to, tied his tongue. Hers, too, he guessed.

He pulled into his underground parking garage, a luxury he paid a huge premium for.

"This is your apartment building," she said, sitting up straighter.

"Yes. I hope you like paella."

After a long, uncomfortable pause she gave him a tentative smile. "It's one of my favorites."

They rode the elevator in a silence that wasn't completely awkward, but unusual for them. He opened his apartment door and took in the scene, trying to see it through her eyes—the table set for a romantic dinner for two. The fireplace ready to light. Candles waiting to be lit. The scent of paella lingering, being kept warm in the kitchen.

"What a wonderful view," she said as if seeing it for the first time. She moved to the window.

It gave him time to turn on the stereo, set to play a classical guitar CD to match the dinner theme. He lit the candles, then the fire. He went into the kitchen to pour them some wine. By the time he returned she'd moved to the fireplace.

"Thank you," she said, accepting a glass.

He touched the rim of his glass to hers. "To the lady in blue. Welcome to my home."

She didn't make eye contact as she sipped. What was going on? Something was obviously wrong, but what?

"Have a seat." He indicated the couch facing the fire. "How was your day?" he asked when they were settled.

"Busy. I walked to the office so I could use the gym. Talked to Fin and my grandfather there for a little while. Went shopping. How about you?"

He'd spent the entire day getting ready for this date, worrying about things he'd never worried about before. "I spent the day awaiting the night."

Everything about her relaxed—her expression, her shoulders, her spine. Had she just been nervous? She couldn't possibly be more nervous than he.

Still the evening dragged. Where was the vibrant Scarlet he knew? Oh, she smiled, even laughed, and touched his hand across the dinner table with her fingertips, but their conversation was less than dazzling. He plied her with work anecdotes and celebrity stories, but she kept her distance. He told her that the vase of eleven roses on the table was for her, to add to the one he'd given her earlier. She thanked him sweetly.

He had no idea how to fix what seemed to be wrong.

When she excused herself to use the bathroom he pushed back from the table, moved to a cabinet and poured two brandies. To hell with Woo U. He wanted Scarlet back.

He heard a slight noise and turned. Scarlet stood a few feet from him—and it was definitely Scarlet. There was fire in her eyes, a flush of color in her face. She'd taken down her hair. She looked like every fantasy he'd ever had of her.

He started to pass her a snifter of brandy, but she held up a hand.

"I'm sorry, but this just isn't working, John."

Nine

Scarlet saw him retreat, his expression distant and self-protective. She hurried to assure him.

"No. Wait." She blew out a breath. "I shouldn't have said it that way. I meant that this…dating thing isn't working for me."

She'd tried all evening to just be his date, but she knew too much about him, wanted him too much. Loved him. And what was she doing, turning him into a better date for other women, anyway? How ridiculous was that?

He set the glasses on the table and took her hands. "Why didn't you say so earlier? I thought I'd really screwed something up."

"Well, actually, you had, but that wasn't the problem."

His brows drew together. "What'd I do wrong?"

"You brought me to your apartment on a first date."

"Where was I supposed to take you? We can't be seen in public."

"You could've gotten creative. You could've thought of someplace to go, something to do where no one would know us. We're not *that* recognizable."

"You're right," he said after a moment. "Bringing you here, especially when we already had memories here…"

"Exactly." She laid her hand against his chest and looked into his eyes. "But that's minor. Truly. Let's be honest. The real issue is that we both know that Woo U was only a ploy to keep us in proximity, an excuse and nothing more so that we could…"

"Sleep together."

She nodded. "We only have two more weeks until… Until. I don't want to waste that time going on 'dates.'"

He scooped her into his arms. She knew where his bedroom was, knew he was headed there. She kicked off her shoes along the way. He said nothing. Maybe he couldn't. She wasn't sure she could, either, she wanted him so much.

It had been nine days since they'd slept together. During that time they'd aroused each other to fever pitch twice—last night and at the country club the week before. This wasn't going to be slow or tender, and she didn't care. Except that sometime she wanted slow and tender.

He didn't wait for her to undress, didn't undress himself. In the bathroom she'd taken off her underwear. When he discovered that, he shoved his pants and briefs out of the way, and drove into her, filling her so suddenly and completely that she cried out.

"I'm sorry. I didn't—"

"It's fine. It's good," she interrupted in a rush. "I was more than ready. You feel wonderful. Incredible." She arched toward him as he moved, finding a strong, hard rhythm. Demand became need. Need didn't want to wait another second. Was that her making that noise? His mouth covered hers, open, wet. He changed the angle of the kiss, groaned into her mouth. She grabbed his hair as the climax hit her, no gentle buildup but a thunderous explosion, matched by him in sound and intensity. Life stood still. Life went on. Life suddenly had direction.

The two other times they'd been together were good. This was phenomenal.

This would never be matched by anyone, anywhere, anytime. She wasn't given to exaggeration, so she believed her own prophecy.

She wrapped her arms around him as he sprawled over her, taking off some of his weight with his elbows, but mostly lying on her like a warm, heavy quilt.

"That was quick," he said, his mouth near her ear.

"And good."

"And good," he agreed, rolling to his side, keeping her in his arms.

She snuggled close, savored the way he stroked her hair. The pent-up tension dissipated. He felt like home.

"Hungry?" he asked.

"Not yet."

"Want to sleep?"

"Hmm." She burrowed closer.

"Let's get undressed first."

She left her eyes closed as he unbuttoned her dress and slipped it off her. She didn't even have the energy to watch him undress. He pulled a quilt over them, wrapped her in his arms, ran his hands up and down her back, then over her rear, along her thighs. When he gently stroked her breasts, she wriggled.

"Relax," he whispered as her nipples puckered. "I just want to touch you. Go to sleep."

She laughed drowsily. "Sure."

He propped himself on an elbow, continuing his exploration. She opened her eyes.

"Spend the night, Scarlet."

"Okay."

His hand stilled for a moment, then journeyed on. A while later, his generosity accepted and enjoyed, she fell asleep in his arms.

He could get used to this, John decided, sitting next to Scarlet. They'd dozed for half an hour, showered together, then decided to have ice cream by candlelight in the kitchen. She was dressed in his robe. He'd pulled on boxers and a T-shirt.

"I would've guessed you didn't even own a T-shirt," she said, spoon in hand. Candlelight flickered across her face. "You look younger."

"Since when is twenty-nine old?"

"Since you dress like you're fifty."

"I do?" He set down his bowl. "In what way?"

"Your suits are boring. And your shirts. And your ties."

He felt too relaxed to take offense. "I think anything compared to your clothing probably seems boring."

"It's an observation, not a comparison."

"I've never felt a need to keep up with the trends."

"You should. You're supposed to be selling cutting

edge, whether it's products or people. You should look like it."

He'd never considered that. "What should I do?"

Even though she didn't rub her hands together, it seemed like she did. "Let me help you choose some new things."

"Put myself in your hands?" The image that came to mind had nothing to do with clothes, but rather the lack of them.

She set down her bowl carefully then moved over to straddle his lap. He was learning just how complicated she was. He'd always expected her to be a sensual, sexual woman, although he'd based that opinion on her reputation more than anything tangible. But he saw shyness at times, too, which surprised him.

This wasn't one of those moments. When it came to sex, she was bold and demanding, but not domineering. A partner in every sense.

"What are you thinking about?" she asked, planting little kisses all along his jaw. "You're so serious."

"Everything that should be at attention is at attention," he countered, with a smile. He had no interest in starting a conversation at the moment.

She dragged her fingers down his cheeks. "I don't get to see these dimples often enough."

"When a clock is ticking on a relationship, there's not much to laugh at." He surprised himself admitting such a thing out loud.

She kissed him, tenderly, chastely. "Let's go to bed."

They blew out the candles, set their bowls in the sink, turned out the lights. In his bedroom they got naked, slipped under the covers and held each other close.

"This is just about sex, John," she said finally. "We can't have more than that."

"I know."

After they made love, she fell asleep. He studied his ceiling for hours, as if the answers to his problems might be written there.

All he saw was that it looked very much as if an Elliott woman would break his heart, after all.

In the morning, her head on a pillow next to John's, Scarlet watched him sleep, his hair mussed, his beard shadowy. She'd slept until nine, not waking once. She couldn't remember a night when she'd slept so well.

Her eyes stung. Anything in life she'd wanted badly enough, she'd gotten, had worked hard enough to get. But no matter what she did in this relationship, she couldn't win.

Betray. Her grandfather's word echoed in her mind.

She eased out of bed, donned John's robe and headed to the kitchen. She hunted for coffee and filters, then fixed a whole pot, not knowing how much he drank in the morning, or if he drank it at all.

At the front door she looked out the peephole to make sure the coast was clear, then grabbed the Sunday *Times* from the hallway. She finished up the dishes from the night before and checked out his refrigerator for possible breakfast food, finding eggs, cheese and English muffins.

At about ten o'clock she heard water run in the bathroom. Curled up on the sofa, she was enjoying her second cup of coffee and the *Times* travel section. A few minutes later he emerged, unshaven but with his hair combed. He'd put on the T-shirt and boxers from the night before. She'd been afraid he would come out in khakis and a preppy sweater or something, dressed for the day.

He stopped in the doorway. A slow smile came over him. "Good morning. How'd you sleep?"

"On my side, mostly."

His smile widened.

"I slept really well," she said, moving her legs so that he could sit beside her, facing her. "And you?"

She offered her mug. He took it, then leaned over and kissed her, deeper than a peck but not an invitation to more. He sipped from the mug, resting his hand on her thigh, rubbing it through the fabric.

"I slept great, thanks. So, what do you usually do on Sundays?"

"If I'm at The Tides I go to church with Gram and Granddad. If I'm in town, I'm pretty lazy. Read the paper. Go for a walk. Have a late breakfast somewhere. Do some sketching and sewing. How about you?" There was so much she had yet to discover about him. She knew his body. She knew his scent, his touch, his laugh. But nothing about his routines, his likes and dislikes. His passions.

"I don't think any two Sundays are the same for me. I play racquetball sometimes, or golf, depending on the season. Visit my parents sometimes. Work at home or even in the office occasionally. Go for a drive. Would you like to go for a drive?"

She wished she could say yes. "Probably not a good idea, John."

His hesitation was barely noticeable. "Right. Well, breakfast, then. I'm pretty sure I have the makings for omelets."

"Do you cook?"

"A little. You?"

"Salads and eggs. And I reheat brilliantly."

"Took a master course in that, did you?"

She recognized the conversation for what it was—avoidance. They were painted into a corner. Don't get too close, learn too much, enjoy too thoroughly. Sex and inane conversation were apparently all they could have. They had to otherwise resist.

"Maybe I should shower," she said. "Then we can fix breakfast together. Then I'll go home."

We can't spend the whole day with each other. The words hung over them as if in neon lights.

"How about we shower together?" he asked, standing, holding out a hand.

Later, she argued against him driving her home. She could take a cab. He didn't think she should be seen wearing what was obviously an evening dress at noon. On the drive to her house he held her hand. She didn't pull away.

"Can we get together during the week?" he asked as they neared her house.

"Definitely. Let's talk later and compare calendars. It'd have to be at your place," she added. "Granddad seems to like being unpredictable these days. I never know when he's coming to town."

"Okay."

They had shared a long goodbye kiss before leaving his apartment, yet she hungered for another.

"Did you expect it would be this complicated?" he asked when they pulled up around the corner from her house.

She nodded. "I'm pretty realistic about most things in life."

"Are you having regrets, Scarlet?"

"None." *Yet.*

"Can I ask a favor of you?"

Her heart fluttered a little.

"If I can arrange a private consultation with my tailor, would you come along and help me choose some new things for my wardrobe?"

"Will you promise not to argue about my choices?"

"No."

She laughed. "Well, okay. That's fair."

"I'll call you later."

The long day loomed before her. She almost wished she'd taken the chance and gone on a drive with him. "Have a good day," she said, then looked around, not seeing anyone she knew. She opened the door.

He just watched her, apparently as tongue-tied as she by the necessarily banal conversation, then he drove off. She walked around the corner. Someone was sitting on her doorstep. She could see fabric through the railings but that was all. Then the person stood, not looking in her direction, as if giving up.

"Aunt Finny." Relieved it wasn't…well, almost anyone else, she waited as Fin met her on the sidewalk.

"I wish I looked that good without makeup," Fin said.

"Oh, right, like you're some old crone. You're only thirteen years older than me."

"That's a lot of years in prime-woman age. I hope you had a good night?"

Scarlet grinned. "I'm relaxed."

"Ah. Lucky you."

"Come inside," Scarlet said, heading to her private entrance. "What are you doing here?"

"Taking your advice. I went for a walk in the park. I've been calling you off and on to see if you wanted to have brunch with me."

"Why didn't you call my cell?"

"I did. It's turned off."

"Oh. Sorry." Probably not turned off but a dead battery, Scarlet decided. "Well, I had a late breakfast, but I'll be happy to keep you company. Did you see Granddad yesterday? He called me up to his office."

"I got the same order, but I had a message sent to him that I'd already left."

"I should've thought of that," Scarlet said, unlocking her apartment door. "I'm trying to figure out who's talking to him about me."

"What do you mean?"

"He said he'd been hearing good things about me. Called me creative and competent. How does he know that?"

Fin frowned. "I haven't talked to him about you."

"You think we have a mole? Someone who reports to him about the goings-on at *Charisma?*"

"Maybe."

Scarlet started to press the message button on her answering machine, then decided against it. Later, maybe. In private. She'd learned her lesson there. "Who could it be? And why is it necessary? Granddad has access to all financial information. Since he's only worried about fiscal profit to declare the winner of this contest, why would he need someone reporting behind the scenes?"

"A very good question." Fin paced the living room.

"I'm going to change. Make yourself at home." Scarlet hurried. She changed into jeans, a T-shirt and a leather jacket, then pulled her hair into a ponytail, added a little mascara and lipstick and was done. She could smell John's soap on her skin, and her body ached comfortably. One area where the man had above average creativity—and flexibility—was in bed. The aftereffects lingered.

"Do you want to go to Une Nuit?" Scarlet asked Fin as they left the house.

"I don't want to go to any family-run operation."

Scarlet smiled. "Hot dog and soda in the park?"

"Sure. Why not?"

A few hours later Scarlet dragged herself home. They'd listed every employee, trying to come up with the name of the snitch. She wished she hadn't said anything to Fin, who didn't need something else to obsess about.

Scarlet made a promise to herself that she would never let her job consume her life as Fin had—easy for Scarlet to say, she supposed, at this point. Maybe when things ended with John, she would dive into her work, too, and not come up for air for a long time.

She hit the message button as she passed by the answering machine, listened from her bedroom to a message from Summer saying she would call Scarlet's cell, four hang-ups, then one from her grandfather.

"Your grandmother and I are coming to the city for the week. She thought I needed to warn you, for some reason."

Scarlet could almost see him rolling his eyes.

"So, here's your warning, missy. We'll be arriving around four. Plan on dinner with us."

Another command performance. Scarlet looked at her watch. Almost four. She needed to call John, let him know....

Why? How would it matter to him?

You just want to talk to him.

Right. And wrong. She had a legitimate reason. They needed to coordinate schedules and see when she could help him with his wardrobe. And she'd expected to spend the night with him at least once. Now they needed a new plan. She couldn't stay away overnight with her grandparents there.

With that rationale in her head she picked up her phone. His number was still on the speed dial.

She hesitated. Why hadn't Summer removed his number? Would a psychiatrist say she was keeping her options open in case things didn't work out with Zeke? Even though she and Zeke were engaged, she'd been engaged before, to John, and that hadn't worked. Maybe Summer was having a life crisis—

Scarlet shook her head. Summer was different with Zeke. Openly happy. Relaxed. Excited. All the things she hadn't been with John, or even before John. Nothing was going to change there, even if Summer changed her mind. And John wouldn't want her back, anyway. Would he? No. Of course not.

She dialed his number, got his machine, but didn't leave a message. She didn't know his cell number.

The intercom buzzed from downstairs. Her grandparents had arrived.

Time to put on a happy face.

Ten

A few days later John stood by while Scarlet pulled item after item from his closet to make room for his just-delivered new clothes and shoes—although he suspected her reason had more to do with removing the temptation of his ever wearing his old stuff again. His new tux and five suits wouldn't be ready for a couple of weeks, but everything else they'd bought could be put away—shirts, ties, jeans, leather jacket, T-shirts, boots, shoes, other casual clothing.

His credit card statement now seemed in line with the national debt, but he had to admit he liked the new look, not flashy but up-to-date.

Not that he hadn't argued with her, starting with her wanting him to use a friend she'd gone to design school with instead of the tailor he'd used all his life, his father's tailor. Somehow—he still wasn't exactly sure how—she'd convinced him to give her guy a try, then decisions were made all around him for a while before he asserted himself with veto privileges and started offering his own opinions. He was happy with the end result, particularly after he finished trying on clothes, when Scarlet locked the dressing room door and they made love, their need to be quiet somehow intensifying everything—scents, sights, the silken feel of her skin, the force of his orgasm.

Or maybe it was the four walls of mirrors that had done that, especially as she'd stripped for him, and he'd had a view of her everywhere he looked, and from every angle.

He went hard at the memory.

"When do you have to be back at work?" he asked her now, coming up behind her in the closet, his hands on her hips, keeping her rear snugly against him.

"Same as usual. One-thirty."

It was the third time this week they'd met at his apartment at noon, and it was only Thursday. They'd also had two meetings at her office about product placements, plus that evening at the tailor's before she had to go home to have dinner with her grandparents. She had to attend the symphony with them tonight, then they were returning to The Tides tomorrow, just in time for the weekend.

Tick tock. His time with Scarlet was slipping away.

They didn't talk about the inevitable end anymore, apparently deciding separately not to bring it up. Sometime soon they would have to, though. Only twelve days until Summer's return.

He'd had lunch delivered before he and Scarlet arrived—corned-beef sandwiches and coleslaw. They sat at his kitchen counter to eat.

Scarlet held a dill pickle aloft. "Make sure you bag your old clothes and leave them with your doorman tomorrow. They'll be picked up around ten o'clock."

He was grateful he didn't have his new suits yet so he didn't have to donate his old ones. They were good suits, with life left.

"And when your new suits are ready, you'll give your old ones away," she added, using her pickle as a pointer.

"Who appointed you queen of my closet?"

She grinned. "Trust me. Once you've worn the new suits and gotten a hundred compliments in five days, you won't miss the old ones a bit."

"If you say so." He had no intention of getting rid of them, but she didn't have to know that. He was taking back a few of the things she'd tossed onto his closet floor today, too.

"Do you have plans for the weekend?" he asked. They rarely planned ahead, usually not even a day, as if they were afraid to. Afraid that they would plan then something would prevent it, which would be worse than not making plans at all.

"I have to make an appearance at JoJo Dawson's party Friday night," she said, "which starts at eight. How about you?"

"I have to be seen at Shari Alexander's opening at the Liz Barnard Gallery."

She frowned. "I didn't get an invitation to that."

"Maybe because at the last opening, you stole Liz's boyfriend."

She met his gaze directly then studied her sandwich for a few seconds as she held it near her face. "I didn't know he was hers. He sure didn't act like he belonged to anyone.

Not to mention he's twenty years younger than she is. Anyway, I wasn't doing anything but flirting a little, *after* he made moves on me. Besides, he was too fussy."

"Fussy?"

"And full of himself."

He wasn't sure what she meant, except they weren't compliments. "I take it I'm not fussy."

She almost snorted. "Hardly."

He wanted her to explain what she meant, but left it alone. They only had a few minutes left before they had to return to their offices. "Want to get together after our respective appearances tomorrow night?"

"Sure." She picked up their plates and carried them to the sink.

He stuck his hand in his pocket, toying with the item he'd dropped in there earlier. After a few seconds, he pulled it out and passed it to her. "In case you're done before I am tomorrow night."

She stared at the gleaming object while she dried her hands, which seemed to take an extraordinarily long time. Then she folded the towel precisely into thirds and hung it on the oven door handle.

"It's a key, Scarlet, not a branding iron."

She took it from him without comment as she edged around him, heading toward the living room. He would love to know what was going on in that head of hers.

"I'll see you tomorrow night," he said as she opened the front door. He wanted her to come back and kiss him goodbye. He stuffed his hands in his pockets, waiting.

She stopped at the door. Her expression seemed to say she wanted to give back the key. A key was symbolic of a relationship deepening in trust and intent, a sign there was a future. It wasn't true here, which obviously confused her, and apparently upset her.

"It's just a key," he repeated to her. "I'm trying to make things more convenient for both of us."

"You keep on thinking that, John, if it makes it easier for you," she said, then she left, closing the door quietly.

So, he really didn't have a clue about how her mind worked. She hadn't been focusing on the same issue at all.

But she was wrong about one thing.

Nothing was making this relationship easier. Absolutely nothing.

Although Scarlet had been taken—dragged—to the symphony and the opera since childhood, she'd never developed an ear for it, nor could she easily distinguish one composer from another. Except for Wagner, that is, especially his *Tristan und Isolde*. Selections from it were on the program tonight.

Still, she would've rather been at a jazz festival or enjoying the pounding beat of a rock concert.

Just before the lights went down she spotted her aunt Finny sitting a few rows ahead with Georges Caron, a French designer old enough to be her father. From their vantage point her real father and mother had a perfect view of their emotionally estranged daughter. Scarlet didn't catch her grandfather looking, but Gram's gaze returned again and again. Scarlet wondered if Fin would ever forgive her parents for forcing her to give up her baby long ago. She'd rarely spoken to them through the years, *Charisma* having become her baby.

On the other hand, Scarlet was glad to see Fin out and about, a rarity for her. Undoubtedly it was a work night for her, an attempt to woo Georges Caron into giving *Charisma* exclusive coverage of his next collection or something. At least it got her out of the office.

Woo. The word stuck in Scarlet's head, along with the other dilemmas crammed in there like a Pandora's box. John had given her a key to his apartment. He was falling for her, beyond sex, beyond their stated intent at the beginning of their relationship. She knew she had to give him up at the end of the month, because of Summer and family image and other things that separately didn't matter a whole lot, but together made it impossible for them to be together.

So…her big dilemma now was whether to end things early with him, before he got hurt, too. She would suffer at the loss of him, but she'd gone into the relationship with her eyes open to that potential. He hadn't. He'd thought it would be a purely sexual relationship, that his heart wouldn't be in danger. She sensed that was changing. Maybe he wasn't in love with her, but he liked her a lot. They had become friends as well as lovers.

It was a dangerous situation for both of them. How had he put it at the beginning—a game with potentially disastrous outcomes? She'd been led by her heart. His mind had presented a more realistic view of the future—then, anyway.

Could she give him up before she had to?

Applause erupted around her as the lights came up. Intermission already?

Georges stopped beside her grandfather's aisle seat and chatted for a moment. Fin stood behind him, expressionless. She wouldn't make eye contact with Gram. Scarlet hated that most.

The Frenchman moved on. It appeared Fin would, too, then she stopped next to her father and in a low voice said, "If there's something you want to know, just ask me. Don't recruit spies."

"I don't know what you mean," he said calmly.

"Liar," Fin fired back before she went to catch up with her escort.

Gram's hands were clenched. Scarlet laid a hand on hers, but her grandmother couldn't even smile.

"Want to attempt the line at the ladies' room, Gram?"

She shook her head. "I see an old friend. I'll go off and visit for a few minutes. Stretch the kinks out, then."

After she left, her grandfather turned to Scarlet. "Do you know what Finola was talking about?"

"Yes. Don't you?"

He looked away, saying nothing. Scarlet didn't know whether he was telling the truth or bluffing.

Scarlet wished John was beside her, holding her hand, defusing the situation. He was diplomatic. He would know how to change the mood. She was too emotionally involved and didn't dare get into it. Instead no one spoke the rest of the evening beyond necessary, polite words.

When she climbed into bed later, she eyed her phone. She knew John's number by heart now. She wanted to hear his voice, but needed to come up with a reason to call....

Food. Food was always a safe topic. She would ask him if she should pick up something to eat tomorrow on her way to his place. He would have appetizers at the gallery, but not dinner, and she wasn't planning to stay for dinner at JoJo's, just to have a drink and show her face.

She dialed. The phone rang four times, then his answering machine picked up. She didn't wait for the beep, but hung up. She glanced at the clock—almost midnight—and tossed the phone out of reach.

Neither of them ever questioned what the other had done on nights when they weren't together, but this was the first time she'd called and not found him at home.

Jealousy reared up. She tamped it down. He'd said they didn't have an exclusive arrangement, but she didn't buy it. He wasn't a player. But she was curious about why he wasn't home yet.

Of course, she had no business calling him at midnight on a work night, when most people were sleeping, and especially to ask a question she could talk to him about the next day. He would see through her ploy. It didn't matter. She didn't care. Let him think what he would.

The phone rang. She leaped across the bed to grab it.

"Hey!" Summer said. "Where've you been all night? I've been calling for hours."

Scarlet settled into her pillows, the phone tucked between her shoulder and ear as she adjusted the bedding. Her disappointment that it wasn't John disappeared. "At the symphony with the Grands. What's up?"

"I just wanted to let you know that we're coming home a day early. The twenty-eighth instead of the twenty-ninth."

One less night. "How come?"

"I'm homesick."

"Really?"

Summer laughed. "No. Well, kind of. Zeke's got a meeting in New York on the twenty-ninth. This is not for public broadcast yet, but he's going to do the music and lyrics for a rock musical."

"Good for him!"

"We think so, too, especially since it means we'd get to live close to home."

"You're going to live together?" Scarlet had assumed they would, but having it confirmed—

"Well, yes. What did you think?"

"Are you coming back to work?" She recalled her grandfather assuming Summer wouldn't return to the job, and had wondered, herself.

"I don't know yet. I'm still figuring things out. Scar?"

"What?"

"You've seemed really distracted every time I've talked to you. This whole month. Longer than that, even. What's going on?"

"Nothing worth talking about."

Static crackled in the silence. "When I get home, we'll catch up. When I can see your face, I'll know whether there's something I should know."

She was right, of course. Nothing Scarlet could say or do would prevent Summer from seeing into her soul—her broken heart at that point, since her relationship with John would have ended.

"Are you planning your wedding yet?" Scarlet asked, changing the subject.

"Not yet. We don't feel we need to hurry. Maybe at Christmas."

"You'll want the fairy tale, I think. It takes time to plan."

"You'll design my dress, won't you?"

Scarlet smiled. "I already have."

Summer's voice softened. "I love you."

"I love you, too," Scarlet managed to say before her throat swelled shut.

"See you soon."

"Okay. 'Bye."

Scarlet could never do anything to alienate her sister. Watching Fin tonight with Gram and Granddad settled that in Scarlet's mind. Family came first. Always and forever.

There would be another man to love someday, she told herself as she turned off her bedside lamp.

Then she lay there in the dark, alone, denying herself the luxury of tears.

Eleven

As director of sales for *Snap,* the celebrity-watcher magazine of the EPH empire, Cullen Elliott had worked closely with John for several years. Almost the same age, they also had a friendship unrelated to the business, having known each other longer than John had known Summer and Scarlet. The men golfed together. Challenged each other. Wagered with each other, too. John liked Cullen and was glad the friendship hadn't been strained when the engagement ended.

"I can't believe you beat me by thirteen strokes," Cullen muttered as they rode the elevator to John's apartment late Saturday afternoon after a long day golfing. "*How* long has it been since you played?"

John smiled leisurely. "I told you. The last time you and I played. October, I think."

"You didn't squeeze in a round or two while you were in L.A. last month?"

"Nope. But conditions weren't the best today."

"Don't be condescending."

John grinned as they exited the elevator and walked down the hall. Usually a prankster, Cullen had seemed to be forcing jokes all day, so John hesitated before he spoke again, not knowing whether he should discuss what he'd observed.

"You did seem off your game," he said finally. "And distracted. Woman trouble?"

"Women," Cullen scoffed. "Sometimes I wonder if they're worth the effort."

"Amen."

"Although I don't ever question it when I'm in bed with one."

John laughed. As he opened the door, an incredible scent rushed at him. Garlic. Basil. Something Italian.

Cullen sniffed the air, making appreciative sounds. "I hope I'm staying for dinner."

Scarlet must be there.

"Sorry, Cullen," John said, upping his normal volume. "Private party."

He heard a soft scampering sound and talked over it, hoping Cullen hadn't noticed. "I'll get that book you wanted."

"Don't I get to meet the chef?"

"I'll check." He walked into the kitchen and looked around. A pot of red sauce simmered on the stove, the source of the mouthwatering aroma. A salad was half prepared. And a pair of spiky black heels lay jumbled on the floor.

He heard a noise from the pantry and headed there, opened the door—

"What are you doing with my cousin?" Scarlet asked in a fierce whisper.

She was wearing a French maid's costume.

John's shock instantly became laughter.

"It isn't funny," she said through clenched teeth.

"From my vantage point it is." He grabbed and kissed her. "I'll get rid of him. Cool your jets, sweetheart."

He shut the pantry door in her face.

"She left a note. Went to the store," John said to Cullen as he passed through the living room on his way to his office. He grabbed a book from his desk. "Here you go. No hurry getting it back to me."

"Feels like someone's shoving a boot against my ass," Cullen said with a grin, heading to the front door.

"What can I say?" The maid costume stayed emblazoned in his mind. The short, short skirt, revealing long, gorgeous legs in fishnet stockings. The low-cut, lace-edged top, exposing inviting mounds he wanted to bury his face in. He could untie her frilly white apron, strip her to whatever fancy lingerie she wore under—

"I'm glad to see you've moved on, you know, since Summer."

John came to attention. "I've become a fatalist."

"Everything happens for a reason?"

"Something like that."

Cullen stared out the window for a few seconds. "Have you stopped loving her?"

I don't think I ever did love her. He didn't say the words aloud, but their truth hit him like a thousand-watt lightbulb. "As you said, I've moved on."

"Mind over matter?"

The way Cullen pushed the conversation, John recognized there *was* something going on with him. "You need to talk, Cullen?" They couldn't now, not with Scarlet trapped in the pantry, but... "We could get together for drinks one day this week."

"Maybe. I'll give you a call." He left.

John returned to the kitchen and opened the pantry door. "Your master awaits."

She eyed him coolly. "My master?"

"If you're the maid, that makes me the master, right?" John admired her in full light. He'd never known a woman with so many dimensions. And he'd never known one so playful, so willing to get into a role just for the fun of it.

He was tempted now to untie the lacy cap on her head and let her hair down. He reached for the dangling ribbons—

"Why didn't you tell me you were golfing with Cullen?"

He lowered his arm, stuffed his hands into his pockets. Obviously she wasn't into her role yet. "I didn't want to wake you this morning. You looked so peaceful."

"You could've told me last night before we went to sleep."

"I could've."

"But?"

"My relationship with Cullen is separate. I don't relate him with your family, even though he is. Why didn't you tell me you were coming over early tonight?"

"I didn't know until after you left your message on my cell, saying to keep the night open for you." She shrugged. "And I wanted to surprise you."

"Which you did." He trailed his fingers down her face, gently, caressingly. "Can I go out and come back in? Start over?"

"First you have to put on your costume."

"Costume?" He hadn't minded the other games, but he'd never had to wear a costume before, either.

"It's on your bed."

"What exactly am I?"

"You're a nineteenth-century duke visiting my master."

"Did I time-travel forward or did you time-travel back?" he asked, pointing to her modern costume.

She ignored his question. "Do you know how men of your stature were treated in the merry old days?"

"With more respect than today?"

His comment earned him raised eyebrows instead of a laugh, then she hooked a finger behind his belt and pulled him toward her. "When a titled man visited, the lady of the house was often sent to assist him in bathing."

"I was born in the wrong century."

Her smile was slow and sultry. "When there wasn't a lady of the house, often a maid was sent."

No joke came to mind. "You're going to…bathe me?"

She dragged his shirt from his waistband and slid her hands up his chest. "I'm going to feed you, then undress you, then bathe you, then have my way with you. And you have to promise not to tell my master, or I could lose my position."

He closed his eyes and enjoyed the feathery touch of her fingers against his skin, although he was more than a little stunned that she had willingly assumed such a subservient role. Another layer of her. Another fascinating layer.

"I think you should go change now, your grace," she whispered. "You can wait in the parlor. I'll bring you some ale to sip while I finish supper."

He'd rather hang out in the kitchen with her, but he acknowledged that anticipation was an appealing part of the game. He expected to stay aroused until she chose to do something about it.

He just hoped his costume wasn't too dorky.

The following Friday, Cade McMann, *Charisma*'s executive editor, stepped into Scarlet's cubicle just as she was about to head to a meeting. Noting Cade's distant expression, she said nothing, especially since he'd come to her. Usually he summoned her to his office.

"You seem to have more influence with Fin than anyone," he said in a low, brusque voice.

"As her niece, not as her employee."

"I don't care which role you assume—whatever works, as far as I'm concerned—but she slept in her office again last night. Obviously I want her to win the contest as much as she does. I stand to win, too. But there's no reason for her to sacrifice everything to it. Someone has to convince her of that."

"If you can't settle her down, Cade, I don't think anyone can."

"I've tried. Short of sending an armed escort to her office to take her home each night, there's nothing I can do. She's the boss. But I'm worried about her."

"So am I." She tapped a finger to her lips. "Maybe I should talk to Uncle Shane."

"They may be twins, Scarlet, but they *are* in competition."

He was right. "Back to square one."

"Just talk to her, please. Better yet, kidnap her for the weekend. Take her to a spa."

This would be her last weekend with John. Summer would be home on Monday. "I can't this weekend, but I'll try to arrange it for the following one."

"Good. Thanks." He turned to leave and bumped into Jessie.

"I'm so sorry," she said, her eyes widening.

Cade frowned.

Looking a little flustered, she turned to Scarlet. "John Harlan is in the conference room."

"Thanks, Jessie."

She hurried away after muttering another "sorry" to Cade.

"She's always hovering," he said, watching her leave.

Scarlet picked up a file folder and stood. "What do you mean?"

"Just that. And she's too eager to please. She volunteers for everything."

"The way our internship program is set up, she's allowed to float from department to department if help is needed, or if she wants to be involved in a particular project. She just has to clear it through me."

"Is she good?"

"She's a natural. As if she's had years of experience instead of just having graduated."

"People said that about *you*."

"They did?" She smiled, pleased. She didn't want to tell the boss to get out of the way, but she did have a meeting to attend. She held up the file. "Is that all for now?"

"Yeah. Thanks."

She was the last to arrive at the conference room, which was populated by most of *Charisma*'s department heads. She was not in charge of the project, so the discussion was being led by the managing editor and the art director.

Scarlet slipped into a chair. John, flanked by members of his own staff, sat across the table. She met his gaze briefly, saw a smile flicker in his eyes, then she tried to focus on the meeting. An hour and a lot of discussion later, the meeting ended. She had no official reason to approach him, plus he wasn't alone, anyway.

She'd been waiting all day for him to call and make plans for their last weekend together. He'd had a lunch meeting, so they hadn't even met at his apartment as they often did. But Summer would be home on Monday. That fact had to be faced.

Scarlet lingered near the conference room in hopes of catching him for a second, but his employees were on his heels and he only got to say a quick goodbye, then he was gone.

Fin was in her office, hunched in front of her computer. Scarlet considered going in and talking to her about getting away next weekend, but decided it didn't matter when she did that, since Fin probably had no plans to interfere with anyway. Scarlet would need next weekend away even more than Fin. A time to mourn.

She returned to her cubicle. It was almost four o'clock. She and John were bad about making plans, but this was ridiculous. It was their last—

She spotted an envelope on her keyboard, her name printed on it. She opened it, unfolded a sheet of ivory-colored parchment. The note was handwritten:

Good afternoon, Ms. Elliott,

Your mission, should you choose to accept it, will begin at 6:00 p.m. You will be picked up from your home and taken to a secret location, where you will be wined, dined and sublimed until Sunday evening. Bring only the basics; no finery required. Lingerie optional but not preferred.

This paper is encoded with a special substance that can read your mind. If you decide not to accept this mission, this note will self-destruct in ten seconds.

10…9…8…7…6…5…4…3…2…1…

See you at 6:00.

Scarlet smiled. A weekend. A whole weekend… To say goodbye.

Twelve

"I know it's unusual to come to the beach this time of year," John said, following Scarlet as she stepped onto a weathered porch. The surf pounded softly. Clouds hid the moon. Distant houses were the only points of light, like earthbound stars.

"It's perfect," she said, leaning her elbows on the rail. "How'd you find it?"

He rested a hand on either side of her, spooning their bodies, sheltering her from the breeze. "Belongs to a client. He's offered it a number of times."

It was late. They hadn't rushed to get there, had even indulged in a leisurely dinner at a roadside diner about an hour out of the city as they drove up the sound toward Rhode Island. They'd lingered in the small, homey restaurant—their first and probably only restaurant appearance as a couple—keeping watch on the parking lot, checking out the new arrivals, even as it seemed an unlikely concern.

After dinner they made the decision not to talk about anything serious while they were at the cottage. Maybe on the drive back, but not now.

Scarlet straightened, forcing him to, and leaned against him, nestling in his arms.

"I haven't been to the ocean in so long, except for The Tides," she said with a sigh.

Until now they'd always been in a hurry, as if someone or something would tear them apart at any moment. For two days, however, they could relax and enjoy each other's company. It was probably a big mistake to end their relationship with a trip to paradise, but he felt entitled to the grand finale. It had been about sex these past weeks—intense, driven sex, with a few quiet or playful moments now and then. That kind of intensity was good in the beginning, but now…?

Now he wasn't guessing anymore. He'd come to believe that Summer hadn't broken his heart at all. Maybe he'd assumed it went with the territory of broken engagements, that he should have been brokenhearted. He *had* been surprised, disappointed and a little humiliated when she called off the engagement, but he'd recovered too quickly for her to have been the love of his life.

But *this* Elliott woman—this one was the heartbreaker.

"Congratulations, John."

He pressed a kiss to her temple. Her hair blew against his skin. "On what?"

"On graduating from Woo U, with honors." She turned to face him and looped her arms around his neck.

He'd been inspired to do the weekend up right, just now realizing he'd been arranging a honeymoon.

And a farewell.

"I think it requires a valedictorian's speech," she said, her eyes sparkling.

He kissed her slowly, gently, thoroughly, savoring the warmth of her mouth, the softness of her lips, the searching brush of her tongue. It was a luxury not to rush, to know no one could arrive unexpectedly or recognize them out walking tomorrow. They could pretend they were a normal couple for once—except they would wear ball caps and sunglasses as a precaution.

"Ah, the ol' actions-speak-louder-than-words speech," she said, snuggling against him, shivering.

"A month in the making. Let's go inside."

The house was typical of seaside cottages, with a nautical theme and blue-and-white decor. Seashells decorated lamp bases and a mirror frame. Interesting glass containers held more, here in the living room, and everywhere, even the bathrooms. The master bedroom's French doors allowed a view of the ocean from the bed. The bathroom held a claw-footed tub with showerhead, and a wraparound curtain on a track.

"Would you like to take a bath?" he asked, still holding her hand.

"Sure."

"Go ahead. I have things to do."

She patted his chest, smiling. "I may have to change your grad status to magna cum laude."

"That would seem to require a more elevated speech."

"Oh, definitely. One that lasts for hours."

"I'll see what I can do."

She laid her hands against his face and kissed him. When she backed away, her eyes weren't smiling anymore but shimmering with something else he could only guess at....

That she didn't want to give up this relationship, either.

Scarlet had debated about what nightgown to bring. Although he'd said in his note that lingerie was optional but not preferable, she'd considered bringing none, then decided that she wanted to tease him with something red and lacy, a reminder. She'd chosen a long gown, which covered her, yet didn't. She'd never felt so voluptuous, her skin warm and damp from the bath, her breasts barely contained by the gown's deep neckline.

Silk brushed her body like a lover's caress as she returned to the living room. Candles were lit; the fire crackled. He'd plunged a bottle of champagne into a condensation-beaded silver bucket and draped a white towel around the neck. Two crystal flutes sat beside it, as well as bowls of strawberries and whipped cream. Quiet jazz played in the background. Pillows were piled on a quilt laid out in front of the sofa. A vase of yellow daisies topped the coffee table, which he'd moved aside. She recalled the white daisies in the master bedroom. He'd set a perfect scene.

How was she supposed to give him up after this? Maybe this last-hurrah weekend was a big mistake. Maybe they should've just kept everything simple. Focused only on the sex. Gotten that out of their systems.

Too late now.

"Did you do all this?" she asked as he came toward her.

He nodded. "I had the refrigerator stocked, too." He cupped her shoulders. "You've never looked more beautiful. And that's saying something."

"You're looking pretty good yourself." She admired his black silk pajama bottoms, and the flesh otherwise revealed. And the sexy mouth. And the gorgeous brown eyes.

Even though the house seemed relatively isolated, he'd drawn the curtains, and she was glad.

"What's wrong?" he asked.

She shook her head. She couldn't ask him if they were making a mistake. She didn't want anything to ruin their time together. "We agreed we wouldn't talk about anything serious."

"Then you need to wipe that serious look off your face."

He was right. She owed him that, anyway. He'd kept his part of the bargain. So she smiled and stepped close and kissed his chest. She felt him inhale, slow and deep.

Guilt settled on her shoulders. She'd started them on this path by going to him. Whatever pain they endured was *her* fault.

"This reminds me of the first time," he said quietly, breaking into her thoughts. "You wore red then, too."

She liked that he remembered. "And you wore black." She slipped a hand down his stomach, his abdomen....

He sucked in air, captured her hand. "I don't want to hurry tonight. Tonight's about romance."

"And memories."

He was quiet a few long seconds. "Let's sit by the fire."

They fed each other strawberries dipped in the whipped cream, and sipped champagne, and touched each other with feathery strokes as the fire provided heat and mood. Words swirled in Scarlet's head, but none she could utter out loud. They were too serious. Too full of what-ifs. Too sad. She had to let the thoughts go, let him fill her world, this world.

He didn't seem in the mood to talk, either. When they weren't kissing, they stared at the fire, hands clasped. But desperation finally seeped in. She toyed with the drawstring on his pajama bottoms, loosened the band and slipped her hand inside. He stretched out and closed his eyes.

She tugged on the fabric, dragged it down and off him, flattened her hands on his shins and kept moving, along his thighs, over his abdomen, up his chest then back down. He arched his hips. She held her champagne flute aloft and dripped the cold liquid over him. He lurched up. At the same time she took him in her mouth, warming him, tasting the champagne…and him. He lay back down, making sounds of need as her tongue sought and savored.

Every muscle was taut. Nothing about him was relaxed. She loved that she made him that way, and that he let her take her time. He made her stop now and then, drew quick breaths for a few seconds, then gave her freedom again for a while. He was a wonder of taste and texture. Heat rose from him. Control slipped away minute by minute, touch by touch, breath by breath.

He stopped her. Moved out of range. Dragged himself up and leaned against the couch. She wished she could sculpt. She would recreate that beautiful, chiseled body still full of need. His muscles were bunched, tendons visible.

She moved closer, laid a hand on his thigh. "Let me finish."

He smiled slightly and shook his head. "I like this feeling. I want it to last. C'mere."

He dove his hands into her hair, pulled her close and kissed her, but it was such a little word for what that kiss was, all open mouth and inquisitive tongue and nipping teeth and hot breath.

"Stand up," he said, low and fierce.

She rose.

"Strip for me."

She let the music guide her. Without hesitation or shyness she moved, turning in a circle, her hips swaying, then finally letting one strap fall down her arm, then the other. Gravity pulled the gown to the floor. She stepped out of it then over his outstretched legs. He grabbed her ankles, applied pressure until she moved her legs farther apart, found her with his mouth and fingers, taking long strokes with his tongue, his fingertips igniting fires, tickling, teasing, letting her need rise, pulling away to let it ebb, then returning again and again.

When her legs started shaking, he pulled her down. She took him inside her, clenched around him. She closed her eyes and arched her back as he drew one aching nipple in his mouth, then the other, cradling her breasts in his strong hands. He was fast losing control, though, she could tell. And so was she. She ended up on her back, somehow, in a maneuver she barely knew happened, and welcomed his thrusts, responded with her own, called out her pleasure, heard his rise above hers. The duet their bodies performed reached crescendo, stayed there, stayed there, stayed there, then slowly, slowly faded.

The beauty of it all made her throat burn and her eyes well up. She wrapped her arms around him, imprisoning him, and refused to let go. They had been well matched physically, sexually, from the beginning. But not like this. Nothing close to this. This was what came when everything was right.

I love you. She said the words to him over and over in her head.

"Fire's dying," he said after a while.

Not mine for you. "We could just go to bed," she said.

"You go ahead. I'll put out the candles and take care of the food."

"We can do it together."

Naked, they moved around the room, eyeing each other, flirting silently. She tried to picture him in fifty years, his hair silver, his smile still wicked. A father. A grandfather. The image came easily. Too easily.

They turned out the lights, walked hand in hand to the bedroom and climbed under a downy quilt. His hands roamed her body, warming her, exciting her when she should've been satisfied.

"Thank you for this weekend," she said, her lips brushing his neck.

"You took the words out of my mouth."

Later she felt him drift into sleep, his body heavy against hers. Only then did she allow herself the luxury of a few tears.

Even so, she had no regrets—except for how it all had to turn out.

* * *

"We have to talk about it," Scarlet said as they drove across the bridge into New York City on Sunday night.

She was right. John wasn't usually one to duck a situation, but he'd been diverting the conversation whenever she even hinted that they should discuss the future—or lack thereof—during the drive home.

They would make love one more time. That was all he knew for sure.

Last night they'd gone to bed and only slept, something a normal couple might do but they never had, because they hadn't had time for such a normalcy. He figured tonight would more than make up for it, sexually. Emotionally, last night couldn't be matched. It had felt good to just sleep together, to wake up in each other's arms and linger in bed.

"So, talk," he said now.

"Summer comes home tomorrow. We agreed to end the relationship when she returned."

"I'm trying to remember the reasons why."

"You know why."

"I know in the beginning we said it was about sex. We figured a month of sleeping together would take care of that." He gave her a quick glance. "It hasn't. Or at least not for me."

"Meaning?"

"I don't want to stop seeing you. Why can't we still meet at my place whenever we can manage it?"

"For sex?" Her voice was strained.

"Not just that." He reached over to wrap a hand around hers.

"It's hopeless, John. We can't ever go public, so why drag out the inevitable any longer?"

"Why not?"

"Because it's too risky. Every time we're together is a chance for exposure. And I'm tired of all the hiding. The sex has been great, but as long as we continue with it, I won't date anyone else. That's who I am. And I'm tired of going places alone. I want a partner. More than ever now, I want a partner."

She shifted toward him, her expression fierce. "Last week when I went with my grandparents to the symphony, Fin was there. They didn't speak to each other, except for Fin to tell Granddad off. It was horrible. My grandmother was so hurt. I've been an observer of their estrangement for years, but never like that. That total public snub. I won't do anything that hurts anyone in my family. I couldn't live with myself if I did."

"How would our relationship hurt your family?"

"It could hurt Summer deeply. Don't you think people might think I had something to do with your breakup if we're seen together this soon after? I'm the one with the reputation, after all. It could seem like I'm rubbing Summer's nose in her mistake—a reminder of how she hurt you. It would be embarrassing for her. I would never, ever hurt her like that, or betray her like that."

"Then maybe you shouldn't have slept with me in the first place."

A few long seconds passed. "I know you're upset, so I'm going to forgive the fact you just put the blame all on me. I was the instigator, I admit, but we both agreed to the terms," she said tightly. "I'm upset, too. But we've been lucky not to be caught. We need to end it before our luck turns bad."

She was right. He'd argued the point because he wanted her to come up with a way for things to be different. An impossible wish.

During the drive they'd agreed she should spend the night with him. It meant her getting up very early in the morning to go home and change clothes for work, but it seemed the best course of action, the path of least possibility of discovery.

He pulled into his parking garage. They got their suitcases from the trunk and headed to the elevator. They hardly took their eyes off each other. He saw in her everything he felt—expectation, need, gratitude and...desperation. In the elevator she went into his arms, pressed her face into his neck then leaned back to look right at him.

He kissed her without restraint, without hope. The doors whooshed open. He would've picked her up and carried her, except their luggage would've gone down in the elevator without them.

He opened his eyes, took a step back...and spotted Summer standing in the open doorway.

Thirteen

Scarlet's world took on a dizzying slant. Her sister stared in horror, in shock, in disbelief. The doors started to close. John slammed his arm against them, keeping them open, then grabbed both suitcases and set them in the hall as Scarlet forced herself out of the elevator.

"Summer," Scarlet pleaded, her hands outstretched. "I can explain."

Summer's face was ghostly pale. She looked back and forth between John and Scarlet. "Did you just spend the night together?" Her voice registered an octave higher than usual.

"Yes, but—"

"Let's go inside," John said, interrupting.

Summer shook her head, took several steps back. "This is the secret you've been keeping from me?

Him?" She looked around wildly. "Was he the reason you didn't come home that night? *The same day I gave him back his ring?*"

"Please let me explain."

Summer held up her hands, warding off the words, then punched the down button. The elevator doors opened immediately and she stepped inside. "And to think I came home a day early because I missed you so much," she said to Scarlet. "And I came here tonight to apologize to you," she said to John, "for treating you so badly."

The doors closed and Scarlet's heart shattered.

"Come inside," John said.

"No."

"She won't be going home. You know that. You won't find her tonight."

"I can't be with you," she said. "I have to go."

"All right." He spoke gently but firmly. "I'll put my suitcase in my apartment, then I'll drive you."

"I'll get a cab." She pressed the down button again and again. "C'mon, c'mon."

"I'll drive you."

"I can't talk to you right now."

"You're mad at *me* for this?"

"No. Yes." She closed her eyes, put a fist against her chest, over her heart. "Both of us. We were stupid to take such a chance just to satisfy physical needs. Stupid, stupid, stupid."

He grabbed her shoulders. "It wasn't just physical for me. Except in the beginning."

What could she say? She didn't want him to know she loved him. She'd kept it secret all this time. She could keep it secret until it died a natural death. She owed Summer that much. "It *was* for me."

"I don't believe you."

"That's *your* problem." She needed to find Summer. To explain. To beg forgiveness. When the elevator opened, she grabbed her suitcase. He followed with his.

"Go away."

"I'm taking you home."

She stopped talking to him. Didn't speak all the way home. Got out of his car and shut the door without saying a word. Words couldn't solve this disaster.

Her apartment seemed cavernous. She looked into Summer's room, saw her luggage still unpacked.

She sat on her sister's bed, brushed her hands back and forth over the spread, then dragged a pillow into her arms and squeezed.

Everything hurt—her head, her eyes, her throat. A cannonball had made a target of her stomach. Her heart pounded a painful rhythm that she could hear in her ears and feel everywhere else.

All these years—all these damned years—they'd never let a man come between them. Some had tried to play games with them, but they'd been open and honest with each other, had avoided misunderstandings and arguments because of that directness.

As soon as she'd realized John was interested in Summer, Scarlet had avoided him, so much so that Summer had asked if she even liked him. At least she had been able to answer honestly that she liked him just fine but that three was a crowd. Still, Scarlet had fallen in love even though she'd fought it every step of the way. Shoved it into a box until that night at his apartment—that amazing night that she'd never dared to hope would happen.

She pushed Summer's pillow against her face and screamed into it. Why had she gone to see him that night? Why had she let herself believe it would be okay to console him, to offer a friendly face? She'd known. In her heart, she'd known nothing good would come of her seeing him alone.

And then she'd convinced herself she only wanted some good memories. Instead she'd hurt the person she loved most in the world, the one who loved her the most, too. Her sister, her best friend.

And it all could've been avoided if she hadn't been so selfish.

Scarlet looked around the bedroom, decorated so differently from her own. Summer's stamp was here—more feminine than Scarlet's. More homey. Her love of antiques reflected their grandmother's.

Will you ever be back?

Will you ever forgive me?

She swiped her wet cheeks with her hands then picked up Summer's bedside phone and dialed her cell number, knowing her sister wouldn't answer it. She waited for the beep.

"Summer—" her throat closed up for a couple of seconds "—there's more to this situation than what you're thinking. I'm not trying to excuse what I did, only to tell you why it happened. Please, I beg of you. If you won't see me in person, at least call me. I…I love you."

She cradled the phone carefully, tossed back her hair and went to her own bedroom, closing the door on the empty room. She wouldn't sleep, she already knew that, so she grabbed her sketch pad and curled up in her armchair, but it was as if the creative forces in her body had imploded, leaving only rubble.

She tossed aside the pad, dragged her hands down her face and leaned her head against the back of her chair. The phone rang. She jumped up, answered it in the middle of the second ring.

"Summer?"

"No, it's me." John.

Scarlet sank onto her bed.

"I figured you'd still be up," he said. "Want to talk?"

"What is there to say?"

"You need to give her time to adjust to the idea."

"If the situation was reversed, I wouldn't adjust."

"Summer will."

"Meaning Summer is a better person than I am." Like she hadn't always known that.

"I didn't say that. You would adjust, too, but it might take you longer."

Scarlet thought she heard a smile in his voice. How could he be smiling?

"But she's in love and happy," he continued. "And she loves you. It's going to be fine. No one else knows, and she won't tell anyone. Except Zeke, probably. You'll get past it."

"How can you be so sure? Why are you so calm about this?" Tears sprang to her eyes.

"I don't think it's worth getting worked up about."

"Not worth—" Scarlet couldn't finish the sentence. "Well, that's easy for you to say, John." Not worth it? "I can't talk to you anymore."

She hung up then curled into a ball on the bed. She'd

regretted some of her actions before—small regrets, like immature choices she'd made or her constant attempts to annoy her grandfather.

But all of them together didn't add up to this.

"Are you in mourning?" Jessie asked Scarlet the next day at work. "I've never seen you wear all black to work before."

Without having slept, Scarlet had gone into the office early, straight into her cubicle, and hadn't emerged.

"Did you need something?" Scarlet asked.

"Touchy," Jessie said, her brows raised. "This came for you. You've sure made somebody happy, to get so many presents." She set a Tiffany's box on Scarlet's desk then strolled off.

Scarlet had no interest in opening a gift from John. She set the box in her desk drawer and went back to work, wishing the time would fly and the lunch hour would come.

At some point during the night she'd realized there *was* someone she could talk to—her cousin Bryan, the only person she was certain could take secrets to his grave. He'd had plenty of opportunities as they grew up to tell on her for things she'd done, misadventures he'd somehow ferreted out, but he never had.

She planned to head to Une Nuit at lunchtime and talk to him, had already called to make sure he would be there. Not only would he keep her confidences, she could count on him for good advice.

All morning long she reached for the desk-drawer handle then jerked her hand away and focused on work again. Every time footsteps approached her cubicle she hoped it was Summer. Scarlet had called her office, thinking maybe she'd come back to work today, but her voice-mail message still said she was out of town.

Finally it was time to leave for Une Nuit. Gray skies and a cool spring shower dampened her hair and matched her mood as she grabbed a cab. When she walked into the restaurant her cell phone rang. She didn't want to step back out into the rain to talk, but she didn't want to miss a call from Summer, either, so she answered it.

"Hey. I hope I caught you in time." Not Summer but Bryan. It could only be bad news.

"In time for what?" She looked around, saw Stash, who headed toward her. "I'm standing inside Une Nuit."

"Damn. I'm sorry, Scarlet. I had to leave. I'm on my way to the airport."

"Something that couldn't have waited until after you saw me?" She was on the verge of panic. She'd needed to talk to someone, and Bryan was her only hope. "What could be so important it can't wait for an hour?"

A few beats passed, then he said, "I got a good line on a saffron plantation in Turkey."

Scarlet sighed. "Okay, I got it. It's none of my business."

"I'll call as soon as I get home, I promise. Or talk to me now, while I'm driving."

Stash stood patiently in front of her.

"I can't. It's too complicated. And too personal."

"I'll make it up to you. I'll call you from the road, if I have time. In the meantime, have lunch on me."

Like she could eat. "Sure. Thanks."

"Later, Scar." He hung up.

She tucked the phone in her pocket, exchanged greetings with Stash, then looked around blindly, wondering what to do next.

"You do not look well," Stash said, concern in his eyes.

"I'm okay. Just not sure what to do, since Bryan's gone." Eating alone was not an option. *Eating* wasn't even an option this time.

"Your cousin Cullen is in the Elliott booth. You could join him." He touched her arm. "At least have some soup. Ginger carrot, one of your favorites."

She nodded, too tired to make conversation. She hoped Cullen was in a talkative mood. She wouldn't mind just listening, being distracted.

"Can I join you?" she asked Cullen, forcing a smile.

"Um." He looked past her, then at her again. "I'm expecting—"

"Me."

From behind her, Scarlet heard John's voice, even imagined that she could feel his body heat.

"So? Three for lunch, eh?" Stash asked cheerfully.

"No." Scarlet stumbled back a step, bumped into John.

Cullen's cell phone rang. He opened the phone then frowned at whatever number was displayed on the screen. He said hello tentatively.

"I...I won't interrupt your plans," she said over her shoulder, feeling John's hand on her back, keeping her steady. She just wanted to fall into his arms. She wanted to be held, and comforted and taken care of and soothed. She'd never wanted that before, never needed to be treated like such a...girl. She even forgot Summer for a moment. She wanted John.

"What?" Cullen asked, his voice rising. "How is she?"

Scarlet focused on Cullen, on the alarm in his voice.

"Where'd they take her?...I'll be there as soon as I can." He snapped his phone shut and stood. "I can't stay."

"What's wrong?" Scarlet asked. Cullen was always in a good mood. Nothing ever seemed to faze him—until now. "Who's hurt?"

"No one you know." He dropped his napkin onto the table. His gaze sought John. "Sorry. I appreciate you coming, but I need to get to Las Vegas."

"No problem. Anything I can do?"

"I'll let you know. Thanks."

He didn't even say goodbye.

John, Scarlet and Stash watched Cullen jog out of the restaurant.

"I wonder if he and Bryan will run into each other at the airport," Scarlet said, feeling sorry for Cullen without knowing why. She'd just never seen him as upset as that.

"Join me for lunch," John said to Scarlet.

She shook her head.

Stash made a quiet retreat.

"We need to talk," John said.

"I can't." She took a few steps, then returned, getting close enough so that others around them couldn't hear her. "And don't send me any more presents."

He looked surprised. "I didn't send you a present."

Then who had? Summer? Scarlet needed to get back to the office. Open the box.

"Goodbye, John," she said, hoping he heard the finality in her voice.

If he said anything, she didn't hear it. She made her way back to her office, pulled out the box, yanked off the ribbon, lifted the lid. Nestled inside was a hinged jeweler's box, which creaked a little as she opened it. Inside was a beautiful gold choker in a modern serpentine design with red enamel accents.

She scrambled to find the card, found it tucked underneath the necklace.

Just a little something to show you how proud I am for what you're doing—with your life and your work.

Love, Granddad

Scarlet put her head on her desk and cried.

Fourteen

Summer stood framed in the hotel doorway, looking only slightly more rested than Scarlet had two days ago at Une Nuit. John was prepared to prevent Summer from shutting the door in his face, but she crossed her arms instead and glared at him.

"How did you find me?" she asked, belligerence coating her words.

It was the first time John thought the sisters seemed alike, the first time he'd seen real fire in Summer.

"May I come in?" he said, not answering her question. He'd pulled strings and greased palms to track down Zeke's Waldorf-Astoria suite.

"I don't think we have anything to say to one another," she said.

"Yeah, we do. It's not like you to jump to conclusions."

"Oh? I have concluded that you and my sister slept together the night we broke our engagement, and have continued a relationship ever since. Is there some other conclusion?"

"The night *you* broke our engagement," he said quietly.

Her face flushed. She started to close the door.

He stopped it. "Look, Summer, I didn't come here to rehash the past—our past—but because I'm worried about Scarlet. I would prefer not to have this conversation in the hall, but if I need to yell it through your closed door, I will. I figure if there were security people in your suite, they would've been all over me by now, so let's just be civilized and talk in private."

After a few moments she stepped back in silent invitation. The enormous suite provided an unparalleled view. He waited for her to be seated, then sat across from her. "Where's Zeke?"

"Out."

"You know, you're acting pretty self-righteous for someone who slept with another man while you were engaged."

"It isn't anything I'm proud of, and you know it. And I also didn't carry on for two months in secret. I told you right away. I also tried to explain. As soon as I met Zeke… You know all this, John."

"You know why Scarlet couldn't tell you about us."

"And you're looking for what from me? Acceptance? Approval?"

"I don't give a damn how you feel about me. I don't want anything for myself." He leaned toward her. "But you need to talk to your sister. She's falling apart. She's not sleeping. She looks…haunted."

Summer pushed herself out of her chair and walked stiffly to the window, but not before he saw concern in her eyes.

"Do you plan to continue your relationship with her?" she asked.

"All I want is for you to reconcile with her."

"Do you love her or were you using her to get back at me?"

He came up beside her. What he felt for Scarlet was more real and powerful than what he'd felt for Summer, but he wouldn't tell her that. "I've learned a lot about myself recently," he said instead, "and I've come to understand what must have happened to you when you met Zeke. I now know I wasn't as engaged emotionally as I should have been or I probably wouldn't have been content with your insistence on abstinence before the wedding."

"And my sister more than made up for that. A good substitute, was she?"

"None of this had anything to do with you." It ticked him off that Summer wasn't seeing the whole picture, but he didn't rise to the bait, knowing it was the only way for her to understand what was happening—that Scarlet needed her. "You learned a few truths yourself when you met Zeke. Do you regret anything?"

She shook her head.

"You caused a small scandal," he reminded her. He didn't need to detail what happened, but it sat there between them, still a little raw. She'd not only ended their engagement in less than three weeks, she'd taken up with a rock star, publicly, happily. It had been a lot for John to swallow.

"You don't think this would be scandalous, John? For

you and my sister to be together? Don't you know how that would look?"

"I'm only interested in getting the two of you back on speaking terms. Nothing else."

"She has hurt our grandfather so many times with things she's done. Not big hurts, mind you, but things done just to irritate him. This would be huge. He might not ever forgive her. And just when they're finally starting to get along."

"There is no reason for Patrick to ever know."

She went completely still. "It's over between you?"

"Yes." Scarlet would never have anything to do with him again. He knew that without a doubt.

Summer was quiet for a long time. John had nothing more to say.

"Does she love you?" she asked. "Does she know what you're willing to sacrifice?"

He slipped his hand in his pocket and fingered his house key, which she'd returned to him by messenger that morning. In the box was a tiny piece of paper. She'd written on it, "Goodbye."

"There's no sacrifice," he said. "It's done. If I can look past what you did, surely you can look past what she did. We were going to end it that night, before you came home. You should've never found out. She was insistent, even though I wanted to continue. She was afraid that someone would catch us, and she would never do that to you."

"I'll think about it," she said after a little while.

But John knew she would go see Scarlet and they would make up. Maybe their relationship would change some, but it had been changing anyway since Summer's engagement to Zeke. John hadn't fully understood the bond between twins before, but he did now. That sibling relationship was like no other.

The distinctive sound of a key card preceded the hotel door opening. Zeke Woodlow came in, saw them together and headed toward them. He put his arm around Summer then extended a hand to John.

"I hope you had better luck than I did convincing her to see her sister," Zeke said.

Any small irritation he'd harbored for the man dissolved. John liked his directness, as well as his obvious love for Summer. "I tried."

"She can be stubborn."

John refrained from saying, "She can?" He'd never seen her stubborn, or pushy, or demanding—all those things he enjoyed about Scarlet. "Those Elliott women," John said instead.

Zeke smiled.

John focused on Summer. "I wish you only the best."

"Thank you," she replied. "That means a lot."

John walked out the door and went home to his empty apartment, where every nook and cranny held a memory of Scarlet Elliott.

Scarlet pushed her sewing machine foot pedal to full speed. She was making new drapes for her bedroom, something that would suit the house from the outside but blend with the contemporary interior. This was the fourth and final panel. In the past few days she'd worked at *Charisma* all day then sewed at night until she fell asleep with her head on the sewing machine table.

As for food—what was that? Toast and tea was about all she could stomach.

She came to the end of the eight-foot-long seam, shoved the pressure-foot lever into reverse, then stopped and snipped off the excess thread, the motion automatic, mindless.

The ensuing silence was horrific. Her CDs must have played out. She rolled her head, trying to relieve the ache in her shoulders, then stood, intending to start up the music again.

Summer was standing just inside the doorway.

Hope gathered strength inside Scarlet, a whirlwind of optimism, a powerful need.

"I came to hear what you have to say," Summer said. "But you have to tell me everything. Don't hold back because you might hurt my feelings." She turned around. "Let's go sit in the living room."

They sat at opposite ends of the sofa. Scarlet didn't know whether Summer was calm or detached, but there was definitely a wall between them, one they'd never had before.

Scarlet didn't know where to start, then finally started with the most critical fact. "I've loved John for about a year now."

A shocked silence blared in the room as if coming from a loudspeaker.

"You have?" Summer finally said.

Scarlet nodded. "I'm not proud of it or happy about it."

"No, I don't suppose you are. But it explains a lot."

"You thought I disliked—" Scarlet began at the same time her sister said, "I thought you disliked—"

They smiled a little at each other. "We haven't done

that in a long time," Summer said. "So, you love him. How did you feel when I told you I'd broken off the engagement?"

"Upset. And confused."

"Why?"

"I thought you were acting without thinking things through, and that you were hurting him unnecessarily."

"You didn't think that now he would be available for you?"

Scarlet shook her head vehemently. "It didn't occur to me. He was in love with you. I never, ever let myself think I had a chance to have him. And I also thought you were just infatuated with Zeke—and the newness of sex. Then when you said you'd never really felt any desire for John, I was angry, too, because you'd been cheating him of yourself, not giving him everything. And he deserved everything."

Summer retreated a little. "You're right. So, actually, you should've been relieved."

"I only knew that he must be hurting. I went to see him that night. To tell him I thought you'd made a huge mistake in ending the engagement, then suddenly we were kissing. And then more." She stopped, breathless, then continued more calmly. "It was my dream come true. I took advantage of it, knowing I would only have the one night. I knew we couldn't have a future."

"Yet it continued."

"Not right away. Not until after you left the country and he returned from L.A. It just grabbed hold of us, Summer. We didn't seem to have any control over it. Like you with Zeke."

"I understand that."

"We decided to take the month you would be gone. It…it was supposed to be a physical relationship only."

Summer's eyes widened. "You never told him you loved him?"

"No. And because we couldn't go out in public, the relationship was more…intense, I think. There were no diversions, no normal dates. We were going to end it the night you showed up."

She nodded. "Now what?"

"Now, nothing."

"You aren't going to see him anymore?"

"No."

Summer went to stand by the window. Scarlet waited.

"Why not?" Summer asked eventually.

"You know why. Because we still can't go public."

"Why not?"

"Because there will be a scandal when that happens, and another scandal when it ends. I'm not putting the family through that." *Granddad just told me how proud he was.*

"Why do you think it would end?"

She'd returned his key. He hadn't called her or come to her to try to give it back. If he loved her, he would fight for her. "I just know."

"You know, Scar, if you'd just been honest with me from the beginning, we could've avoided all this."

"That's not true. You know it's not true. You would've been just as hurt and angry—maybe even more so. You would've hated both of us, John *and* me."

"I meant way back, when you first fell in love."

Scarlet joined her sister at the window. "How could I tell you? What was I supposed to say? He preferred you."

Summer pressed her fingers to her eyelids. "Maybe you're right. And maybe you're right about not telling me after the first night you shared. I certainly would have thought that John was using you to exact revenge on me."

"He wasn't."

"I realize that now." Summer stared at the street. A long time passed, more than a minute. "I think you should go after what you want," she said at last, her voice wavering just a little.

Scarlet felt her jaw drop. "You're kidding."

"No."

"How can I do that? What would everyone say? The Grands—"

"They always liked John."

"How do I explain it? People will talk. I'll need to have answers."

"The four of us will go out together. Be seen. Let them talk. Who cares?" Summer's whole attitude changed, from her posture to her voice. She exuded strength and certainty.

Hope returned to Scarlet with a vengeance, but practicalities still got in the way. "I can't do the public thing unless John and I have a future together. A long future."

"So find that out first and go from there."

"I can't believe how generous you're being. If the situation were reversed—"

"You would do the same thing."

Scarlet put a tentative hand on her sister's shoulder. "It was so hard keeping this a secret from you."

"Don't do it again." Summer's eyes welled. "I know a lot has changed for us, but nothing can destroy our bond unless we let it. Regardless, Zeke is a part of my life now."

"I know that, Summer. I do. I think I felt left behind. Maybe a little jealous. You were so in love and so happy. And I envied you leaving your job, even if it was only for a month. It was only for a month, right?"

"I don't know yet. I doubt it, though. I'm finally going to do it, Scar. I'm going to make a career as a photographer."

There were no more questions, no more revelations. They went into each other's arms and held tight.

"I love you so—"

"I love you more than—"

They laughed shakily.

"So, why don't you show me your design for my wedding dress," Summer said after wiping Scarlet's tears away.

"Have you set a date?"

"We're talking about one. But I'm willing to wait until it can be a double wedding."

More hope wove its way through Scarlet. A different kind of hope. One with John as the focus. "You'll want the big, splashy wedding, Summer. I won't."

"Yes, you will." Summer's smile was all-knowing.

"It's never been my dream."

"Until you fell in love." She hugged Scarlet. "Show me my dress. And yours."

She found the sketch of Summer's dress and brought it out to her. Scarlet didn't want to jinx anything by pulling out the sketch of her own dress—the wadded-up paper she'd rescued from her trash can at work with her impetuous design. She hadn't redrawn it on clean paper. Nothing was certain yet.

"Oh!" Summer traced the lines of the gown with her

fingertips as if the fabric were in her hands. "It's exquisite. And exactly what I want."

"I know."

Summer shoved her, and they laughed.

"I'll hire someone to sew on the beads and crystals, but I want to make it for you," Scarlet said.

Summer nodded, tears in her eyes. She grabbed Scarlet in another big hug.

"Can you stay tonight?" Scarlet asked.

"Don't you want to go see John?"

"Not tonight. Tonight I want to be with you." She stepped back and smiled. "And sleep."

"I'll call Zeke and let him know."

Scarlet wondered if they would ever have another night like this, just the two of them. Probably not.

The thought colored the rest of the evening, giving everything they said and did a bittersweet edge. Who could have predicted they would undergo so many changes in just a couple of months?

Where would they be a year from now? Would they even be in the same country? When Summer and Zeke decided to have children, would Scarlet even get to know them or would they always be on the road?

She pictured her sister pregnant, smiling serenely. Summer would take motherhood in stride.

As for herself, Scarlet couldn't bring up the picture as readily. Maybe because her future wasn't as settled as Summer's.

But that was all about to change.

Fifteen

The Elliott helicopter swooped over The Tides, preparing to land. Scarlet took in the vista from above—the enormous turn-of-the-century home rising near a bluff overlooking the ever-changing Atlantic. The elegant circular drive, so often filled with cars. Her grandmother's glorious rose garden and perfectly manicured lawn, fragrant and inviting. Many a game of hide-and-go-seek had been played in that garden and countless touch football games on the lawn.

Hand-carved stone stairs led down the bluff to a private beach where Scarlet and Summer had whiled away warm July days and hot August nights as they talked about boys and life and their parents, desperately trying to keep them alive as their memories threatened to fade.

Scarlet's relationship with The Tides was complicated. A haven but occasionally a jail. Gram the peace-keeper; Granddad the warden. Summer the diplomat, and Scarlet the rebel…until this past year, when she'd stopped waging war with her grandfather. It had felt good, too. Incredibly good.

She gathered her courage as the helicopter set down gently, then she thanked the pilot and battled the wind generated by the blades as she ducked to race across the helipad.

For the first time ever Scarlet had ditched work.

She ran into the breezeway and entered the house from the side entrance. Heading straight into a powder room tucked under the staircase, she brushed her hair, straightened her clothes then went in search of her grandparents, who were expecting her and had surely heard the helicopter arrive.

Her stomach hurt from stress and anticipation as she walked through the house, expecting to find them in the solarium enjoying the morning sun. They sat on a love seat, heads close together, speaking quietly. Maeve touched Patrick's face lovingly. He laid a hand over hers. Their tenderness after fifty-seven years of marriage was enviable.

Scarlet closed her eyes; drew a slow, deep breath; let it out just as slowly then walked into the room. "Good morning," she said, bending to kiss each of them. "Thank you for sending the chopper," she said to her grandfather.

"It sounded urgent."

"Have you not slept in a month, then?" her grandmother asked, concern creasing her face.

"I'm okay." Scarlet thrust a box at Patrick. "I can't keep this. It's beautiful, Granddad, and exactly the kind of necklace I would wear, but I don't deserve it. I don't deserve what it represents, what you said in your note. You won't be proud of me once you hear what I came to tell you."

He frowned. "You've caused no gossip since that hoodlum a year ago. And I've been assured that you've become invaluable to *Charisma*."

"Just because he rode a motorcycle doesn't make him a hood—" Scarlet stopped the automatic argument. She couldn't lose her temper now. "It doesn't have anything to do with my job," she continued, forcing herself into control, then remembering he had a snitch in place at the magazine. "Who's your source there, anyway? Fin hates being checked up on."

"Fin's paranoid."

"Patrick," Maeve chided.

"Well, she is. I don't check up on her. I've no need to. I can see the numbers any time I choose. I asked Cade how Scarlet was doing. At least he speaks to me. Finola chooses not to."

With good reason, Scarlet thought.

"Sit down, missy. Tell us what's on your mind."

She pulled up a chair, grateful to sit. "I've been seeing John Harlan."

Her grandmother's eyes opened wider, but that was her only outward reaction. Her grandfather's expression darkened, the calm before the storm.

"Seeing him? What does that mean?" he asked coolly.

"Dating him."

"Sleeping with him?"

"Yes." Okay. The worst was out now.

"For how long?"

"A month." She decided they didn't need to know

about the stolen night, the first night a month earlier. That could only hurt all those involved.

"Does your sister know?"

Scarlet nodded. "She wouldn't have, but she came home a day early and saw us together. We were going to end it that night."

Her grandfather shoved himself up. Scarlet stood, an ingrained response. She wasn't wearing heels this time, so she couldn't meet him eye to eye. He seemed to tower over her.

"I thought you'd grown up finally. How could you do that to your sister? Betray her like that?"

He'd used the word before—betray. Even though Summer had forgiven her, it still stung, especially since she'd worked so hard to change. *Had* changed.

"I couldn't help myself," she said quietly. "It's no excuse. I know there'll be penance to pay."

"Couldn't help yourself?" he roared. "Animals can't help themselves. The weak can't help themselves. You're a strong woman who knows the difference between right and wrong. This is wrong, missy."

"I know."

He walked away.

"I'm sorry," Scarlet said. "I know I've disappointed you. Both of you." She dared a look at her grandmother. "I didn't mean to hurt Summer. She's the last person on earth I'd ever hurt."

"But you did, *colleen,*" her grandmother said.

She could bear being a disappointment to her grandfather—that was nothing new—but not Gram. Scarlet wanted to stare at the floor. Instead she kept her head up.

"Why are you telling us?" he asked.

Scarlet hated that she'd put that tone in his voice that said she'd failed him, had fallen short of his expectations. "Because I'm in love with him."

"You mean you have every intention of going public with this? Humiliating your sister?"

"Summer is fine with it. As for going public, I don't know for sure. I just wanted you to know, in case."

"Does he love you?" Gram asked.

"He hasn't said so."

"Are you looking for my blessing?" Granddad asked, as if dumbfounded. "You think I would—"

"Quit prowling," Maeve said, interrupting. "Sit yourself down. You're not helping."

"I should help this?" he queried righteously, but he sat anyway. "I should make her comfortable?"

"Yes, I do believe you should, dearie."

Scarlet was grateful to sit again. "I didn't have anything to do with their breakup."

"Of course you didn't," her grandmother said, patting her hand.

Scarlet grabbed it as an anchor. "I do want your blessing, Granddad. I don't know what will happen. Maybe all this would have been unnecessary. But I can't even begin to hope things can work out with John unless I know you accept it."

"Give my blessing, you mean."

She nodded.

"And if I won't?"

She met his gaze directly. "I won't see him anymore."

He sat back, his brows raised. "You would give him up?"

"I'm not the girl I was. I've grown up. I appreciate

all you did for Summer and me after Mom and Dad died. I'm sorry it took so long for me to show you."

The room held no clock to tick during the long silence that followed, but the sound seemed to reverberate inside Scarlet's head, anyway, a time bomb determining her future—she hoped. John still had to have his say.

"You have our blessing," he said at last.

As if a nuclear blast hit her, she fell into her grandmother's waiting arms, wishing she could control the relief that spilled out in huge, gulping sobs, but finally just giving in to the overwhelming emotions. She felt her grandfather pat her back a few times.

"You'll make yourself sick," he said, obviously uncomfortable with Scarlet's tears when he was accustomed to arguments.

He stuck a handkerchief in her hand. She grabbed hold of his hand, too, then shifted from her grandmother's arms into his. "Thank you," she whispered shakily. "Thank you so much. I'll try to handle it in a way you can be proud of."

"I am proud, missy. I've always been proud. You've got a good bit of myself in you. It's why we butt heads. I expect you'll go far in the company, maybe even run it someday."

Scarlet used his handkerchief to dry her cheeks and blow her nose, stalling. She tried to smile. They had, after all, taken Summer's request for a leave of absence well. "About that…"

He raised his brows.

"No matter what happens with John, my plan is to stay on at *Charisma* until the end of the year—when Fin wins the contest," she added pointedly. "And then I'm going to try my hand at designing full-time."

"You couldn't have saved that bit of news for another time?"

"Might as well put everything on the table at one time. Deal with it and move on."

"That sounds suspiciously like a motto of your own," Maeve said to him.

He smiled, then shrugged.

"You'll be wanting to take the helicopter back right away, *colleen*."

"Yes, Gram. Thank you." She stood.

Patrick stood as well, and passed the jewelry box back to her. "I haven't been more proud of you than now, Scarlet. Wear it with pride. My pride. You've become your own person. It needs recognition. No more tears," he added in mock horror.

She laughed. Then she left to find the man she loved.

Sixteen

Late that afternoon John closed his office door, shutting out the normal workplace noise, which seemed suddenly chaotic. He'd been sure he would hear from Scarlet as soon as Summer forgave her—or whatever they did to make things right again. He'd certainly expected their reconciliation by now. He didn't know what to make of Scarlet's silence.

He checked the time. She would still be at work, but just barely. He dialed her number, got her voice mail, waited for the beep. "It's John." Did he really have to identify himself? "Give me a call when you have a minute. Thanks."

If she didn't call back before he left the office he'd try her home phone, then her cell. He needed to know what was going on with her, wanted to tell her a few things, too.

His private line rang. He let it ring twice, his hand on the receiver. "John Harlan."

"Hi, it's me."

Scarlet. Message received. He dragged a hand down his face and relaxed into the chair.

"Thanks for calling." He held back from bombarding her with questions because he wanted to see her in person, to know for himself how she felt. He needed to talk her into meeting him somewhere. "Did you and Summer settle things?"

"Yes."

He waited, but she didn't add anything. "Well… good."

"John? We need to talk."

"I agree. That's why I called you."

"You—" A pause, then, "When?"

"Just now. Isn't that why you're calling?" he asked.

"No. I wanted to let you know I'm sending you an envelope by messenger. You can read what's inside and think it over and get back to me."

"Why don't we just meet?" he asked.

"Everything will be clear when you get the message."

At this point in their relationship she'd decided to play a game? Why wouldn't she just talk to him? "All right, Scarlet. I'll get back to you."

"One way or the other, please?"

He wasn't sure what she meant but figured it would work itself out. "Okay."

"See you later," she said, almost turning it into a question, but not waiting for an answer before she hung up.

He called the doorman in his apartment building to

say he was expecting a delivery and to call him as soon
as it arrived. Someone rapped sharply on his office door,
then opened it without waiting to be invited.

"Got a minute, son? We need to talk."

John stood to greet his father, aware of how ominous
those words sounded, echoing his own to Scarlet. It was
not the best day in his life.

Scarlet shook out her hands to help calm her nerves
then strode lightly across the sumptuous hotel suite to
the door. She viewed the room from the entry. The small
fortune she'd paid for one night in the two-room suite
at the Ritz-Carlton was worth it. A table for two was
already set by a window overlooking Central Park.
She'd arranged for a memorable meal from the hotel's
award-winning restaurant, Atelier, everything from
beluga caviar, to bluefin-tuna-and-artichoke salad, to
herb-crusted rack of lamb with spinach-and-ricotta
gnocchi, to the decadent final touch—warm molten
chocolate cake with caramel ice cream.

It was a meal meant for a celebration. She'd even
met with the master sommelier to choose wines for
each course.

Now all she needed was John.

She paced the room, caught a glimpse of her reflection
in a window in her fitted black sheath, black-satin-and-
rhinestone high heels and her mother's pearl-and-
diamond necklace and matching earrings. She'd never
worn them before, had saved them for a special occasion.
She couldn't imagine an occasion more special.

The mantel clock struck six. Any moment now, he
would arrive.

She was scared and anxious and exhilarated.

She wandered around the room, moved dinner plates half an inch then back again, straightened perfectly aligned silverware, picked up a wineglass, held it to the light then set it down again in precisely the same spot.

She walked some more, stopped at a window. A siren blared, an everyday sound that pierced the quiet hotel room then stopped nearby.

In the sudden silence the clock chimed the quarter hour.

She went into the bedroom to find her watch, double-checking that the clock was right. It was.

Six-thirty came. Anxiety played hide-and-seek in her head.

Six forty-five. Worry joined the game.

The phone rang. She almost came out of her skin. He was delayed, that was all, and calling to say so.

"Hello?" She heard herself, breathless and hopeful.

"Miss Elliott?"

Not John. "Yes."

"Were you ready for room service?"

"I need a little more time." She'd arranged to call them when she was ready but had told them it would probably be about 6:15 p.m. "I'll get back to you as soon as I can."

"Of course, ma'am. Good evening."

Scarlet blew out a breath. Where was John? She had left nothing to chance, had even called to alert him about the envelope. Yet now she was left staring at the hotel door, willing him to knock on it, but only silence echoed back.

Seven o'clock came. Eight. She dimmed the lights and curled up on the sofa.

He wasn't coming. Apparently he'd thought about what she said in the note and made his decision. Except

that he'd told her he would call, one way or the other, and
he hadn't, and he was usually a man of his word. Maybe
she had been too pushy, her expectations too high.

But he'd called her, too, wanting to talk. He'd said
so. What did it all mean?

At 9:35 p.m. she cancelled room service and turned
a chair to the window. Headlights dotted the nightscape
as a steady stream of traffic passed below her. They
blurred into ribbons of light, red one direction, white the
other. Horns honked. Life went on.

But not hers.

Why didn't he want her? Was she too much trouble?
Maybe she'd been too bold, undermining him as a man.
Maybe he thought she was high maintenance, someone
who brought too much drama into a life.

Okay, perhaps she'd stirred his life up a bit, but she
wasn't exactly a drama queen. She hadn't changed him.
He was still the cool, calm person he'd always been.

Maybe that was the crux of the problem. She was too
intense. He was too calm.

Fire and ice. Good for a sexual relationship, but not
for life.

She looked blindly around the room, aching disappointment drifting around her. How could he just blow
her off like that? Okay, so she hadn't exactly encouraged
him since Summer had discovered them, had actually
discouraged him. But he was big on courtesy. He should
have at least let her know he wasn't coming. He'd said
he would. He was a promise keeper.

Unless he was hurt?

She laughed at the idea, the sound brittle, and wished
she'd ordered the champagne to be delivered anyway,

so she could toast her fertile imagination. She'd seen *An Affair to Remember* too many times, that was all. And she'd heard the siren earlier. It had stopped right in front of the hotel, hadn't it? Had it been an ambulance?

"Right, Scarlet. He was looking up at the hotel and was hit by a car on his way to meet you."

Frustrated, she walked to the window again and looked out, resting her forehead against the cold pane. She just wanted—needed—a reason for why he wasn't there, that was all. Because her imagination put him in an ER somewhere, bleeding, barely conscious, calling her name, since in some way it was preferable to him ignoring her.

And that was her wake-up call. She grabbed her things, then left for home, wanting nothing more than to curl up in her own bed, and never see the Ritz-Carlton again.

In her car she rolled down her car window, felt the chilly air against her cheeks as she drove, trying to erase the memory of the night. The short drive seemed infinite yet instantaneous.

She reached the town house, hit the garage door opener and saw the spot where she usually parked her car, gaping and empty—a glaring reminder of the state of her life.

Some welcome home.

John clutched a Glenfiddich on the rocks in one hand, his first of the night, and a ring in the other, not missing the irony of the déjà vu moment and wishing he was as close to drunk as the other time.

A small scraping sound made him turn toward the

front door. Something flat and white lay there. He slipped the ring into his pocket, walked over, picked up the envelope. Finally, Scarlet's envelope had arrived. Instinct made him open the door, because the doorman would've called first.

A woman stood at the elevator, her back to him. There was no mistaking her this time.

"Scarlet?"

She spun around. "I thought—" She hesitated, looking confused. "Your car is gone."

"It's in the shop." He waited for her to approach, but she didn't, which confused him.

The elevator door opened. She looked into the empty cavern then didn't step inside. The doors closed quietly.

He opened the envelope and pulled out a piece of paper. "Obviously we don't want the same things," she'd written. "Goodbye."

That was it? The big mystery in the envelope? She'd already said goodbye, when she'd returned his apartment key. So what did this goodbye mean? She'd changed her mind, but had changed it again now?

"Come in," he said.

"I'm comfortable here."

Leave it to Scarlet to make everything a challenge. She kept him on his toes, and fascinated.

John held up the paper. "I don't understand. What do you want that I don't?"

She pushed back her shoulders as if gearing for a fight. "I had *wanted* to continue our relationship."

"Continue in what way?"

"As we had. Just spending time together."

As they had? "In private?" he asked, bewildered.

"Snatches of time during the week when we can find it? Maybe an overnight on Saturdays? An occasional week-end away?"

"Yes."

He studied her. It wasn't what he'd expected. He'd thought she would either cut him off altogether as a sac-rifice to her relationship with Summer or demand more of him. At the least he'd figured she wanted the one last time in bed they'd missed out on when Summer had sur-prised them.

"Nooners?" he asked, stepping into the hall.

She flinched. "Everything the same as it was the past month," she said. "Except this time with everyone's blessings, which they gave."

"Even Patrick?"

"I think he's mellowing."

John didn't have time to consider the implications of that. "No," he said.

Silence stretched out for days, it seemed.

Finally, she jabbed the down button.

A door across the hallway opened, and his neighbor looked out, eyeing the both of them.

"Sorry, Keith," John said to the man, taking quick strides to get to Scarlet before the elevator arrived and she was swallowed up by it. His neighbor shut his door.

In a low voice he told Scarlet, "I'm not interested in that proposition, tempting as it sounds on a base level."

"I figured that out already. *No* has no alternate mean-ing. This conversation is over."

"Not even close. But unless you want my neighbors to hear the rest of it, I suggest you come inside." He put his hand on her arm, urging her toward his apartment.

"There's nothing more to say."

"There's a helluva lot more to say."

After a moment she went along, although jerking free of his grasp. She walked directly to his couch then didn't sit.

"May I take your coat?"

"I won't be here long." She crossed her arms.

"I'm missing a piece of the communication puzzle, Scarlet. You act as if I should've known what you wanted."

"If you'd shown up at the hotel, you *would* know."

"What hotel?"

She looked at him as if he'd lost his mind. "The Ritz-Carlton, of course."

"Of course," he repeated without any understanding. "I was supposed to be there, I gather."

She narrowed her gaze. "It was in the envelope."

He glanced at her note. Had she lost her mind?

"Not that envelope," she said. "The other one."

"This is the only one I've received."

"But…it was delivered five minutes after we talked. The courier confirmed it."

He stared at her, baffled. "At my office?"

"I told you it was coming." Frustration coated her words and stiffened her body.

"My father dropped by. He needed to talk to me about some family business, so we went to the bar next door. I called my doorman and told him to contact me when—" He paused. "I assumed you would send it *here*."

"I didn't."

He'd gone crazy sitting at the bar with his father, waiting for a call. "Sit down, please. Can I get you something to drink?"

She shook her head then perched on the sofa, her hands clenched on her knees. John sat in a chair opposite from her. He wasn't alone in his loss for words. A comedy of errors, he thought, but not funny at all.

"You're wearing one of your new suits," she said after a moment. "It looks nice."

Avoidance. She was trying to regroup. What was in that envelope, anyway? "You were right. I got compliments."

"Why are you still dressed up?"

He ignored her question. "What was in the other envelope, Scarlet?"

"A key card for a room at the Ritz."

"And when I didn't show up, you thought I'd left you high and dry? Do you know me at all?"

She looked out the window. "I didn't know what to think," she said into the quiet.

"Why didn't you call?"

"Because if you were intentionally ignoring me, I didn't want the humiliation."

"So you came in person instead?" He smiled at her, not quite following her logic but appreciating how much her emotions were involved.

She stood abruptly. "This isn't going anywhere. Let's just call it a day. A month. Goodbye, John." She headed toward the door.

"When I said *no* earlier," he said, following her, "I meant I wasn't interested in keeping the status quo."

She continued toward the door.

"What I *am* interested in," he said, "is a full-time, publicly acknowledged relationship."

Her steps slowed.

"I love you, Scarlet."

She stopped and turned around, her gaze meeting his, her expression one of guarded surprise. He caught up with her and slipped his arms around her, but still she didn't speak.

"This is the part where you say you love me, too." His heart thudded. He was taking a leap of faith, based on everything he'd seen in her eyes this past month, heard in her voice, felt in her touch. Still, he wouldn't know until she said—

"I fell in love with you a year ago," she said, her voice just a whisper, as if she were afraid to admit it.

"A year ago? But—"

She put a hand over his mouth. "As it turns out, you're not the man I thought I fell in love with."

A year ago. She fell in love with me a year ago. The unbelievable words kept repeating in his head. Then it hit him that she was speaking in the past tense. "Meaning what?" he asked.

She toyed with his lapels. "You were an ideal, and I loved the ideal without really knowing the man. I hadn't seen below the surface until this month. Now you're real. And now my love is real, too."

The world righted itself. He pulled her closer, needing to hold her, needing her arms around him, squeezing tight. She pressed her face against his neck.

"Do you want to know when I started falling in love with you?" he asked, loving the feel of her breath against his skin, warm and unsteady, hinting at intense emotions. "At the country club. In the conference room. When you stopped me from making love with you on the table. That hadn't been my goal when I got you in there. All I wanted was a kiss, but things escalated. You do that to me."

He stroked her hair, enjoying the soft sound of pleasure she made as she snuggled closer. "There is much more to you than I'd guessed, and I want to know it all. I want *you*."

He kissed her, long and lingeringly, putting everything into the kiss that he felt, feeling everything back from her. Then he framed her face with his hands, keeping her close.

"I want you to marry me, Scarlet. Will you marry me?"

She smiled; her eyes welled. "Yes," she said, then repeated it in a stronger voice. "Although one little problem does stand in the way. Summer wants to have a big, splashy wedding. Those take a while to arrange."

"What do Summer's plans have to do with us?"

"She'd like to have a double wedding."

It didn't surprise him. The twin bond was a powerful force. It did surprise him that they'd discussed it already. "And you? What would you like?"

"I want to marry you, period."

"But you'd like to do the spectacle with your sister. The Cinderella thing."

"I promise it won't be a three-ring circus. It'll be tasteful and classy and—"

He kissed her, this time without restraint and with the intent of getting her to think about something else— him. Them. Now.

He lifted her into his arms and carried her to his bedroom, as he'd done the first night she'd knocked on his door. In his pocket was the ring, nothing as simple as a diamond. She was a complex woman who needed a different kind of engagement ring, something untraditional, something with flair.

He'd chosen it yesterday, had tried not to think about what he would do if she said no. He would've fought for her, though. Fought hard.

He wouldn't give her the ring tonight. Tonight he would give her himself, and let himself just enjoy her. Tomorrow, though, he would find a creative way to present the ring to her. His magna cum laude graduation from Woo U wouldn't go to waste.

"I love you," she said, reaching for him.

There was so much yet to say and do and discover. But it started and ended with one truth. "I love you, too," he said. "Forever."

* * * * *

Silhouette®

Desire®

Coming in May from Silhouette Desire

SECRET LIVES OF SOCIETY WIVES
All the money in the world
can't hide their darkest secrets.

The series begins with

THE
RAGS-TO-RICHES WIFE

(SD #1725)

Metsy Hingle

She was Cinderella for a night—swept away
by a rich, handsome stranger. Now
she was pregnant and about to become
that stranger's blackmailed bride.

On Sale May 2006

The drama continues in June with
The Soon-To-Be-Disinherited Wife
by Jennifer Greene.

Available at your favorite retail outlet!